REAP Not The DRAGON

DEBRA KRISTI

Ghost Girl
publishing

Reap Not The Dragon
Age of the Hybrid: Book Two
Copyright © 2014 by Debra Kristi

All rights reserved.

Published in the United States by Ghost Girl Publishing, LLC.

ISBN-13: 978-1-942191-04-9
ISBN-10: 1-942191-04-9

Cover design artwork by Adara Rosalie
Book layout by Book Cover Corner

Kristi, Debra
Reap Not The Dragon / Debra Kristi. – 1st ed.
Visit the author: http://www.debrakristi.com/

SUGGESTED READING ORDER:

To discover more about books by Debra Kristi, visit her book page where you can explore worlds and characters to your heart's content: http://www.debrakristi.com/all-books/

....

For updates about new releases, as well as exclusive promotions and giveaways, sign up for Debra Kristi's Insider's Club mailing list here:

http://eepurl.com/T3tNv

For my mom,
the most amazing woman I've had the privilege to know.

REAP Not The DRAGON

Book 1 in the Age of the Hybrid series
A Mystic's Carnival Story

DEBRA KRISTI

Tis Death's Park, where he breeds life to feed him.
Cries of pain are music for his banquet.

- GEORGE ELLIOT

Welcome

Mystic's Carnival. You may have heard of it—the name has been whispered in quiet conversation, mentioned in folktale. Many believe it does not exist. Let me assure you, it's as real as the air around you. If you are lucky or so in need, you may be among the few who come to know the wonder of this mysterious destination. It is not your average carnival. No, not at all. The show of twirling lights, motor rides, and funny sideshows never moves, never sleeps, and can never, ever be found unless so wished by the carnival herself. Is she a living, breathing entity? I'll let you be the judge.

Follow now, if you will, into the story, and let our characters introduce you to the splendor of their world and the mystery that can only be found at Mystic's Carnival.

Safe travels, weary reader~

WRECKED

Death was always the same. Not the people or the place or the circumstance. That changed from one stop to the next. Each one unique in its own special way. But Sebastian had come to understand his calling in the past few weeks and now recognized the signs for what they were. Always present. Always pulling. And always overwhelming with the constant stench of death. His own personal calling card.

Sebastian had lost count of the number of souls he'd helped cross over since embracing his Reaper half. He'd fought his destiny. Feared being an icon of death. A messenger of doom. All to help Kyra escape purgatory. For her, he'd do it again in a fluttered heartbeat. She was more than his best friend. He'd come to crave everything she brought to their relationship. Even the rage of her dragon.

Things were different now, though. He understood a Reaper's value.

And Kyra…well, she didn't remember him. At all. Of course, he would change that. Very soon. First he had to get past Marcus's damn barrier spell. Sebastian clenched his fist and imagined it slamming into Marcus's jawline.

Damn Marcus for taking Kyra.

Damn him for keeping her from Sebastian.

And damn him for escaping the Reaper.

Sebastian stood beside his second stop of the day. If he had a choice, he'd be at Marcus's door right now, but the opportunity to get away from his father's prying eyes had yet to present itself. So he tried to behave like any young trainee and assessed the scene. The asphalt spread before him, a dark and crumbled highway to the unknown—at least, unknown to most who found themselves in need of Sebastian's services. He knew exactly where it led.

An empty aluminum can lay at his feet. With slow and deliberate intention, he knelt down and retrieved the evidence. Beer. Sunlight reflected off its silver surface as he spun it with his fingers, then shoved it at the boy standing before him. Right into his hands. Hands covered with blood.

"Think that last drink was a good idea?" Sebastian cocked his head, indicating the mangled mass of metal sitting on the edge of the road. Steam poured out from under the crushed hood.

With an air of indifference, the boy peered at the crumpled can, then over at the crash site, before looking back at Sebastian. The boy's face resembled an emotionless wax dummy's. He shrugged. "Ehh. Sure, the car is a loss, but I have insurance, and look at me! Not a scratch. Pretty awesome. Right, dude?" He casually brushed the dirt from his shirt. "What the...?" He swatted harder, trying to remove the foreign object stuck to the front of him.

Sebastian knew it was wrong to feel the way he did, but he loved when this happened. A slow, deliberate grin spread across his lips. "That's my claim ticket, Lance." He soaked up pleasure in the taunting, the boy's name lingering on his tongue, dragging out slow and deliberate.

A tarot card clung to the fabric of the boy's shirt like a second skin—a dancing skeleton prancing across his chest. Sebastian watched blatant confusion and fear spread across the boy's face.

Deep valleys curved the flesh across Lance's forehead. "Hey man. Do I know you? How do you know my name?" His voice wavered.

"Think you made it out unscathed? You might want to take a closer look." Sebastian motioned to the wreckage across the road.

Lance flinched at Sebastian's words. He whirled around, faced the ruin, and darted forward. Sebastian knew he rushed for proof, proof of the Reaper's lies. There were always types like Lance. Never trusting. Always needing to see for themselves. There was no denying the moment Lance discovered the truth about his misguided assumption. The quickened pulse, the bulging eyes, the sudden intake of breath—something Lance hadn't yet discovered he no longer needed.

Crumpled behind the wheel in the driver's seat slumped an exact duplicate of the teenager standing near Sebastian. Only the one in the car looked like a broken doll, staring into a void. He was nothing but an empty shell, left vacant by the confused, departed soul.

"But—I—Sophie—" Lance stammered.

"Yes." The word dripped like castor oil from Sebastian's lips as he stepped behind the addled soul. He dropped his fingers upon the boy's shoulder in one quick tap before trailing them down his upper back.

Lance broke into a dance of shivers and shudders, then twitches. A mask of dread slipped in, contorting his face and replacing his once-handsome features. A small cry escaped. He turned, glued his gaze on Sebastian, an overwhelming plea swimming in his eyes. "What did you—?"

But it was already too late.

He was sinking, melting down through the ground. Pulled by long, dark, shadowy arms, reaching and grabbing and dragging him under.

Sebastian watched until the boy was no more, knowing his destination was hot and horrific. Excruciatingly torturous. With Lance gone, Sebastian breathed deep, relief blooming in the knowledge the worst was done. He crossed the road, circled the battered car, and approached the passenger side. There she waited, as if in limbo, completely unaware. He placed his hand upon the open window with the tender touch of a grief counselor. The trigger. Her eyes popped open and her head snapped up.

The girl was still dressed in her high school cheerleading uniform and wore Lance's senior ring on a chain around her neck. "Where am I? What happened?" Her voice cracked, rough and dry, from a throat in need of water.

Sebastian opened the car door and laid his palm out before

her, awaiting her hand, and offering to help her from the vehicle. "Come. Let me help you."

Her gaze glanced over him, then over the scene again. "Where's Lance?"

Sebastian knelt, dropping down to the car's front seat level so they could meet eye to eye. "Don't worry about Lance. Let's take care of you. Will you allow me to help you, Sophie?"

Sophie sucked in a deep breath. Her frail body teetered backwards, and then slowly swayed upright. Slipping her hand into Sebastian's palm, she stood, stepped away from the car, and stared at her Reaper. Her eyes widened. "Your aura, it's so..."

Sebastian warmed her hand in his and looked away.

She tilted her head. "You don't want to know. Do you?"

Fact was, he didn't. He feared the knowing. Feared what his true aura would say about him. As long as he was ignorant of the truth, he could avoid admitting ugly truisms. "You can tell me if you want to," he said, "but it won't do me any good. I'm fated to what I am. I doubt the color of my aura will make a difference one way or the other." He looked past her and his shoulders sagged. "Are you ready?"

Sophie followed his gaze, her own falling on the broken sight behind them. "Oh!" She turned back, allowed Sebastian to pull her away, away from the wreckage. "I didn't make it, did I?" Her voice was weak and tearful.

Sebastian understood. She didn't want to see the mangled remains in the car. In the last few weeks, he'd heard the request many times. They rarely wanted to know, usually preferred to remember themselves as they'd been before, not how they'd ended up. He agreed it was for the best.

"I'm sorry, Sophie." He glanced at her from beneath a fall of dark hair. "Do you need some time to let it sink in?"

Her eyes glazed over and she stared into the distance. "No." As if chilled, she crossed her arms and hugged herself. Sebastian supposed it was an attempt at self-comfort. "My parents," she whispered.

He brushed his hand back through his hair, shifted his weight.

"It'll be hard, but they'll be alright. Trust me. If you'd like, I'll have someone check on them."

Sophie glanced up, her eyes bright with tears. "Would you do that?"

He jerked back. "Me?" He searched her face, looking for any doubt, but found none. "If that is what you really want, I will."

Sophie nodded. "It is. Thank you."

Sunlight bled through the trees lining the roadside, and Sophie's blonde hair reflected the light in ribbons of gold. It's a shame she moved on so young, so senselessly, thought Sebastian, but it was only his job to make the transition as painless as possible. He didn't get to choose who or where or when.

He pushed her hair away from her face and hooked it behind her ear. The action reminded him of Kyra. How many times he had wanted to brush back her wild red hair. Bravery had never backed him long enough to make that move, and now—

He shoved his personal baggage aside and focused on Sophie. "Are you ready?" he asked again.

She blinked and responded with a nod. It was a shaky nod. One that wasn't sure of its true answer, yet wanted to be.

Warmth spread across Sebastian's skin and the edges of his lips curled up into a smile. "Don't be afraid. It's a far better place you go. Makes this place look like detention."

Sophie's face glowed, garnished with a genuine smile and silent laughter. Sebastian smiled, too, outwardly if not committed inwardly. His heart warmed, taking pleasure in the small moments of his quotidian. Sebastian let his hand drop to her elbow. "In all seriousness, you've led a good life, Sophie. You have nothing to fear." He looked over her shoulder to a spot beyond human visibility.

The turn of his body, the pull of his arm, all signaled Sophie to follow his lead. Extraordinary light seeped through the opening, expanding in broad beams of intense emotion and illumination. It pushed forward and out, opening like no other door. Each time Sebastian lived the experience with someone, the crossing, their door, and what waited beyond was unique. Fingers of warmth, acceptance, and love slipped through the gateway, swirling and winding their way toward Sophie. Dazzling ambassadors to take her home.

Through the opening, Sebastian caught glimpses of the new world to which she was destined. One bathed in unimaginable beauty. So intense was the sight, he could barely look upon it. But it was not meant for him. It was never meant for him. This invitation was for Sophie and Sophie alone. Sebastian raised his hand to shield his eyes.

Verse swept through the gap, melodious words wrapping around Sophie, pulling on her like a magnet. Sebastian felt it. Felt the tenor in the music and felt her emotion. He felt it all. All part of his supernatural gift, the pros and cons of being a Reaper. He was only a Minor Reaper, but he was still bestowed with the gifts and abilities to guide his clients. His father preferred to refer to the clients as marks. Sebastian never thought of the individuals he helped that way. With some exceptions, such as Lance.

Sebastian felt the fervor flowing from the gate, urging Sophie onward. "You should go. You'll be fulfilled there."

When Sophie turned and looked back, she glowed the most brilliant color of rose. She threw her arms around him and hugged him tight, and then pulled back. "My parents?"

"Consider it done."

"Thank you. You're a good man." She turned to leave, then paused, looked over her shoulder. "I didn't get your name."

Sebastian fought a grin and looked down. He casually pointed to the bottom edge of her skirt. "It's Sebastian, and it's been a pleasure."

She glanced down and saw the tarot card plastered an inch above her hemline. "Is that your card? Will I find your number scribbled on it somewhere?"

Sebastian laughed. "You should be so lucky."

"You can't blame a girl for trying to get to know her savior."

His face drooped, body chilled to dry ice temperature. He'd dragged this one out too long. A savior? He was anything but. Sophie needed to go—leave—move on. With the sweep of an arm, he motioned for her to start. She sighed, but didn't argue. In slow, forever steps, she moved forward as Sebastian had suggested, on through the door and into the brilliance of the light beyond. Exceptional radiance, something he'd never know, flowed all around her, painting her the illusion of the perfect angel.

Three steps in, her footing faltered. She stopped and called back, "Maybe I'll see you again…in your next life?"

Sebastian's lips twisted into a smirk. "Nice thought. Highly unlikely. There's no place for my kind where you're going." He watched her face drop and knew it was time to terminate the conversation. "Goodbye, Sophie." He turned and walked away.

Circling the heap of twisted metal, Sebastian crossed the road. He walked directly to the man waiting where the asphalt met dirt. Waiting and watching. Tall and lean, the man stood supporting his weight against the side of a telephone pole. His hands were shoved deep into the pants pockets of his gray wool suit. Only one button was done on his jacket, and he wore his hat on a slight tilt. A slap-n-stick name tag clung to the breast pocket of his jacket. Bold red letters ran across the top saying Hi! My name is. Scribbled beneath that in black was the name Mr. Smith. Sebastian thought the tag and the man wearing it—his father, actually named Mortifier—were a grim joke. Nevertheless, the air vibrated around him, hinting to his importance.

He grinned at Sebastian. "Awfully sweet on that one. Spent far too much time."

Sebastian huffed. "You're entitled to your opinion. I see nothing wrong in treating them with a little kindness and respect." He glanced back at the gateway. Sophie was barely visible; the light practically enveloped her. As it should, he thought. That was her home now. The doorway flashed with unmeasurable luminosity, collapsing the window inward, closing off the passageway.

Sebastian turned back toward the man in the suit. Mortifier stood straighter, fixed his jacket as he regarded Sebastian. "I've been doing this a lot longer than you. You would be wise to heed me every now and then."

"I'll keep that under advisement…Dad."

Mortifier laughed. "You do have a spark about you. Reminds me of someone." His hand flipped, exaggerating his meaning. It was unnecessary. Sebastian knew he'd meant himself.

His father punched a finger toward the middle of the street. The slightest of marks was now visible where the boy had descended. It left a scar upon the asphalt for all to see. Sebastian looked, but said not a word.

Mortifier circled around, placing himself between the site and Sebastian. "What did you do to him, before you sent him off? You added something to that unique cocktail of yours, didn't you?"

Sebastian's gaze slowly raised to meet the superior Grim Reaper's, his jaw tight. "I simply sent him where he was meant to go. You saw the kind of life he led."

Something gleamed in his father's eyes as he stared down at Sebastian. "Yes, that I know. But you did something else. Tell me."

Sebastian looked away, his face falling like a shadow slipping in at sundown. He didn't want his father to see his shame. Not now. Maybe not ever. He wouldn't understand. Mortifier felt fine sending souls to Hell. Ending life on the spot. Not Sebastian. And what he had done was worse. Not only had Sebastian tortured the man without reason, he'd crossed the line, violated the guy's privacy. Digging into people's secret thoughts and turning what he'd found against them was wrong. He hated himself for it.

"I gave the guy a nightmare," he said. "Plucked his most isolated fear and set it free to ravage his mind. I'm not proud, okay?"

Deep, dark, deranged laughter burst from Mortifier's lungs. It filled the air around them and the sound of glass crackling responded from the wreck across the road.

"Enough! Stop it," Sebastian demanded.

His father, now quiet, took on a nefarious, loaded grin. "It's quite marvelous. Don't you see? You are exactly as I had hoped." He reached out to touch Sebastian, only to have Sebastian smack his hand away.

Sebastian notched his fists on his hips and narrowed his eyes, staring at his father. "All I can see is that you made me into a freak.

A freak that was never meant to be." He raked his hand through his hair, took a deep breath. "I don't fit in anywhere. And I never will. Mom doesn't want me because of what I am. And you want me for all the wrong reasons." He turned in a slow circle and let his hand fall. It slapped across the front of his leg. "Don't think I'm here for some father-son bonding session. That couldn't be further from the truth." Sebastian stepped back onto the road. "Now if you'll excuse me, I have somewhere I need to be. Made a promise to a girl."

Mortifier took a step after him. "Best not be the dragon. You were supposed to take her. You know that, boy. She was your mark." His voice was stern, tinted with discontent.

Sebastian's back and shoulders tensed. He whipped back to face his father. "Her name is Kyra, and no one's reaping her, so back off." He pushed up his sleeves.

Sharp pain cut through Sebastian's calves and kneecaps, crippling him and dropping him to the ground. Every pebble pressing into his palms symbolized another minute, another day slipping between him and Kyra. Too much time had already been lost in finding the magic necessary to break Marcus's barrier.

Sebastian grated his teeth and, with great force, pushed himself up. Standing as if gravity willed him flat on his belly. "Why in Death's name did you do that?" He practically spat the words at his father.

Mortifier studied his nails. "Just a reminder of who the boss is around here. Stay out of dragon business, boy. And stay away from her. It's not time."

Sebastian brushed the dirt from his hands. "When will it be time? According to you, the time is never right." His father, this whole training process, was infuriating. Sebastian rubbed his forehead. "You said two hundred souls would satisfy my initiation requirement. That was the last one—two hundred exactly. I'm done. Free to go. You don't get to tell me what I can and can't do anymore."

Mortifier shook his finger. "Not so fast."

Sebastian's shoulders slumped and his hands hooked low on

his hips. "What now?"

"You will have more freedom now, but that doesn't mean you're not on probation. You're still a Reaper. You must still reap, or back under supervision you will go. Abuse your freedom, and back under supervision you will go. Mess where you don't belong…" His father assessed Sebastian. "Understand me?"

"I get it. I don't like it, but I get it." Sebastian turned, put his father behind him, and didn't look back. He'd made a promise, and he wasn't one to break a promise. Not even to a girl he'd never met before today.

He heaved a heavy breath. How much trouble can a bunch of Reapers swing down on me if I follow my own path to Kyra?

"You're not ready, boy," Mortifier called behind him.

Putting one foot in front of the other, Sebastian trudged down the empty road, the next town his destination—home to Sophie's parents, and as it so happened, Marcus Blackall.

2

COFFEE

Sebastian walked into town with two thoughts on his mind: defying his father and finding Sophie's parents. He started with the simple one first—Sophie's parents. It was a relatively easy assignment for a Reaper. When you deal in death, you tend to get a built-in tracking system. Like a GPS for souls. The walk took longer than expected. Night had turned into morning. Cars now motored down the streets and people moved along the sidewalks, starting their day. Sebastian stood outside a five-story apartment building, looking up.

Just great, he thought, and rubbed the back of his neck. People living in tight quarters. Too many bodies, too little space. Harder to pinpoint exact locations without walking the halls, getting close. Something he wasn't looking forward to doing. All the confined emotions would be insufferable. He hated his nobility, keeping a promise under such conditions. Through the double glass doors at the front, he could see a handful of mothers sitting around chatting while their children played in the lobby. Double great.

A giant yawn bound from his body and he stretched his arms wide. Sleep had evaded him lately, leaving him tired and cranky, hardly feeling up to the chore asked. An image of Kyra wrapped in nothing more than a robe standing beside Marcus flashed through his memory. It hit him fast. Dagger to the heart. He hated recalling that day. The day she no longer remembered him, their friendship, or the kiss they'd shared. The day she chose Marcus over their forgotten friendship.

He closed his eyes and rubbed his temples. This thing with Kyra—he wasn't going to let go, but couldn't let it consume him, either.

Stupid Reaper rules—damn them to hell. And Marcus, too. He could burn and take his infuriating magical barrier with him.

Taking a deep breath and exhaling slowly, Sebastian gazed down the block to the bustling coffeehouse. A cup of hot java to get the synapses firing, that's what he needed. Help focus his thoughts and get him back on his game. Could he suffer the coffee-seeking crowd in his less-than-ideal condition? He was willing to give it a try. Likely to be less people in the coffeehouse than in the building housing Sophie's parents.

He moved to the center of the sidewalk and headed down the street. When he hit the alleyway at the edge of the apartment building, he paused, looked down the path. Someone stepped out of a door several feet away. There must be another entrance into the building there—a quieter one. The side door off the alley could be used to get to Sophie's parents. It was unlikely mothers with little ones populated both entryways. He would try the side door later.

Content with the plan, his thoughts returned to caffeine, and his stride moved straight toward the small storefront with the elaborate Java Time sign hanging in the front. An odd familiarity floated over the place. The shop sign drew his gaze like a corpse in the middle of Sunday Mass. The sign showed time slipping down the front in the form of a melted clock face. Coffee poured from a tipped pot jetting out of the used brick wall. In a stream of neon lights, the liquid flowed over the clock and into a chipped cup braced above the entrance.

The sight birthed a déjà vu feeling. The kind bound to happen in his vocation. He'd been so many places, seen so many things, in order to help the departed move on. He was likely to run into some of the same things occasionally. Then there were the memories. So many memories. Passing through the air, through the ether, through him, as his clients transitioned. Occasionally he would confuse which memories were his and which were not.

The door handle was warm to the touch, many hands having

already used it this morning. He pulled open the door and stepped into the comfortable atmosphere the shop provided.

Within, people huddled in tight little groups. They sat at tables and sofa and chair groupings alike. Burning in a small hearth at the back corner was a fake crackling fire. The walls closed in with an exuberant collage of chipped and mismatched tea and coffee cups and saucers. Burnt yellow paint washed the walls, while thick weaved rugs softened bare spaces beneath rich wood furniture.

Sebastian was third in line and although he didn't need to, he studied the menu. They didn't have what he needed, but he knew what he wanted. Straight black coffee. It would do. It had to. If only he could nab a vial of Talia's Spiritual Peace from the cupboard back in his trailer at the carnival. A splash of that in his coffee, and all these emotions and memories would cease to bother. He rubbed at his forehead, wished for silence—internal silence.

The feeling he'd seen this coffee shop before continued to nag at him. He glanced at the fireplace. Hmm, pretty damn sure he'd never been here before. Then the memory dawned. He'd looked through the front window on his way to find Kyra that morning, the morning she'd forgotten him. It had been a brief glimpse, but that was all he'd needed to imprint the image. He remembered.

He was minutes away from Marcus's condo. His chest heaved, inner conflict solidifying. The moment he'd walked into town, he should have recognized the tells. He'd known he was close, but had no idea how close. He'd been too focused on Sophie's parents. Now all he could think about was Kyra. He missed her, worried about her, and should have checked on her sooner. But he hadn't had the answers then. The answers that would get him past Marcus's doorway and the magical barrier the jerk had somehow erected. Now he'd lost an entire month to the search and his father's demands. Sebastian clutched at the side of his leg. The thought of Kyra with Marcus...

Imagery started to flicker through his mind. He tried to stop it short. Didn't want to go there. Didn't want to think about Marcus touching her, kissing her. His chest tightened and his heart ker-thumped. He needed to calm down. The tips of his fingers had begun to burn with anger. All the emotion welling inside had him wanting to reap, collect Marcus's soul. He should have. Should have collected it the first day he saw Marcus, when he'd been called to complete that very task. Had he done his job correctly, none of this would have happened.

"Dammit, Kyra." He ground his teeth and muttered the words under his breath. As much as he didn't want to blame her, part of him did. It was her heroics that had gotten them here. If only she hadn't saved Marcus that day.

If only.

So many if-onlys loomed in their past. He dragged his fingers through his hair, knocking the hood of his jacket back. He didn't care. Felt no need to hide here.

Soon he would put this behind them. He had what he needed now. Marcus could no longer keep him out. His hand slipped into his pocket, wrapped around the gift from Talia. The small charm in his pocket would get him through the doorway at Marcus's. Talia had guaranteed it.

Stepping to the front of the line, Sebastian placed his order and then moved to the side to collect his coffee. Ready immediately, a young man handed him an open-topped cup and moved away, busy with other preparations. Sebastian reached around to grab a lid. After snapping it in place, he turned to leave, only to smack right into another body. "Oh, hell. I'm sorry." Sebastian wiped the coffee from his jacket, then looked up. Involuntarily, he sucked in his breath. Kyra stood in front of him, an innocent twitch of a smile gracing her face.

He blinked hard. She still stood before him. Was it true? Marcus had let her out of the house?

She reached past him to the counter and grabbed a handful of napkins. "Don't be sorry. It was completely my fault." Separating one napkin from the pile, she dabbed at the coffee spill on his hand.

A warm tingle raced through Sebastian's body. He knew he had to say or do the right thing to hold the moment and make it count. Problem was, he had no idea what the right thing was. "I'm the one that turned in to you. Did I get you? With my coffee, I mean?"

Kyra batted her eyelashes and her gaze traveled across Sebastian's features. "I think I escaped unscathed. You're lucky." She laughed.

Sebastian raised a brow. "No doubt." He didn't know what to think of this version of Kyra. Without her memories, she'd been molded into a completely different person. Did Marcus have the power to make her into anyone he wanted? If he successfully rewrote her, what would happen to the girl Sebastian had known, and—? He couldn't finish the thought. His body began to burn again. Burn with desire to tear Marcus to pieces.

"I have a confession to make," Kyra said. Sebastian blinked and returned his focus to her. "I came over here because I saw you."

Sebastian's blood cooled and his muscles eased. "You walked over to see me?"

Her face lit up and it looked like she was trying to hide embarrassment. "Well, yeah. You're the guy who came to my home that day, aren't you? The one who knew me before?"

Sebastian's heart beat heavily in anticipation of where their conversation might lead. He could only imagine positive things. Still, he'd take it slow, be cautious. "Yes. I came looking for you. I was told, not so politely, to leave you alone."

White lips pressed firmly together and Kyra released the breath she'd been holding, spewing a minute trail of dragon smoke from her nostrils, so small it was barely noticeable. Sebastian squinted at the curious sight. He watched Kyra cough, her hand reaching to cover her mouth, then reaching back toward the counter to grab a napkin she used to blow her nose.

"Excuse me," she said, discarding the napkin in the trash. "I'm really sorry about that." She reached out, letting her fingertips graze the top of his hand, setting off a chain reaction. His blood vessels snapped and sizzled with pure adrenaline, shaken with excitement. "First, I caused your drink to splatter, then I coughed in your face." She blushed. "Would you have coffee with me? You aren't in a hurry, are you?"

Sebastian couldn't recall where he'd needed to be. Not with Kyra asking him to stay. Nothing was more important than solving the issue of his fervid dragon girl. Although, he suspected she wouldn't think of herself as anything needing to be fixed, figured, or solved. Not this new version she'd become. "Nowhere to be. I'm all yours."

"Great! I'm just going to get my coffee. Why don't you grab us a table?"

While Kyra wandered to the back of the line, Sebastian found a table near the wannabe fireplace. It crackled and popped, similar to the real thing, without giving off a lick of heat. Sebastian's instincts told him to sit facing the door. Always on guard, he watched his exits, covered his back at all times. Except this time. This time he sat facing the register and watched Kyra. In his world, it had been forever and a week since he'd seen her. In reality, it had only been a month, if that. All he wanted to do was absorb every angle, every fiber that was her. She didn't turn, didn't look back. Not until her order was complete. She was playing it cool. Or maybe she didn't care as much as he liked to think. He couldn't be sure. While she waited to the side for her coffee, she chanced a quick glance, and that was something, enough to build hope.

Sebastian liked to think the power of old Higgins's sacrifice was working to their benefit. Working to help bring Sebastian and Kyra back together after the ordeal in purgatory. Sebastian owed him big time for all he'd done. They both did. Someday Kyra would remember, and when that day came, she would be gutted with guilt. She'd even missed the old bird's funeral.

He took a sip of his coffee and leaned back, stretching out his legs and crossing them at the ankles. Settling deeper into his seat, he took in the full view. Kyra looked good, healthier than she probably had in a while. At least Marcus was taking care of her physically. Sebastian jerked and shook the unwelcome imagery that had begun to play in his head.

"Do I have something on me?"

Sebastian looked up at Kyra. He could feel the tension creasing in his brow and at the corners of his eyes.

"You were staring at my outfit. Did I spill something on it?" Kyra looked down to her white pants in search of anything out of the ordinary.

"I was just taking in the change. That's all."

Kyra set down her coffee and a small plate of fruit, then took a seat. She sighed, glanced over her attire, and then casually slid the plate between them. "You're welcome to have some if you'd like. I didn't get a chance to eat yet." She slung her burgundy bag over the arm of the chair. As she did, the long curls she'd taken the time to twist into the locks of her red hair bounced with the swing and sway of her body. Sebastian found himself hypnotized.

He should have broken away from the Reapers, checked on her sooner. Should have found the witch, Talia, quicker, or pushed Marcus harder to see Kyra. Now she had been reprogrammed like some sort of minion. If he didn't know her better, he wouldn't even recognize her. This feminized corporate look was a long rock toss from the leather jacket rebel he was used to Kyra sporting. All this time, he had feared pushing her away in the process of saving her. That was nothing. Losing their friendship didn't matter, not when compared to losing Kyra as an individual.

He wanted to grab her by the arms, shake her, slap her across the face and tell her to snap out of it. If it didn't work, he surely would lose her after a move like that. He took another sip of his coffee and waited.

The silence between them grew. It didn't bother him. He enjoyed the simplicity of her company. That quiet—it was more than they'd had in a long while.

Kyra gazed at him, her lips tugging to the side. "I take it I didn't used to dress like this?" Sebastian didn't answer right away. He watched the muscles in her face, looking for any nervous tic. "You did know me before, didn't you? Before I lost my memory?"

Sebastian sat up and leaned forward. "I've never seen you dress like this. Jeans and cotton were more your thing."

"Oh." Kyra chewed on her pinkie nail, her gaze fluttering down to her cup. "I can't remember her. The girl I was." She shifted, stared out the side window, and her eyes shimmered. Thinking it the start of a tear, Sebastian began to reach across the table, but reconsidered and pulled back. She wiped her eye. "I work today. This is my work attire."

"You have a job?" This interested him. Marcus had seemed so protective of her that night. Like a child unwilling to share his toy. Now he was letting her out of his sights long enough to work a day job.

"I work at the bank." She motioned across the street. Sebastian balked. Kyra's face fell into a frown. "Your expression says it all. Not the old me?"

"It's fine. If that's what you want to do with your time. Is it what you want?" Sebastian asked.

"That's the problem. I don't know what I want. When I woke up in the hospital that night and Marcus was there by my bedside, I thought he was the answer. Thought he was the answer to everything. Especially after the nurse told me he'd been there with me the whole time, waiting. They told me I was out for two days. Two days! He never left the hospital in all that time." Kyra sighed, looked down at her hands. "Things are different now. I don't remember my life, but I feel things. Does that make sense?" Kyra looked down, picked at the protective sleeve on her cup. "Sometimes I get glimpses of things, and I think—I feel they should mean something to me."

Feelings were something Sebastian had more than his fair share of experience with. His own, and those of every other soul who had passed through his Reaper half. He thought he understood but couldn't be sure with a hundred percent certainty. But glimpses, that caught his curiosity. Could she be experiencing fragments of memories? "Mind expanding on that?"

She took a deep breath. "Marcus is fine. Marcus is…Marcus, you know?"

"Not really, but continue." He was pretty sure they both had extremely different opinions regarding Marcus.

Kyra fidgeted, stirring her coffee. She spoke in a metered tone. "He's nice and I enjoy his company, but I don't feel like he's letting me discover who I am more than trying to direct me. He got me a job at the bank where his buddy works so I'd stop complaining about being bored. I'm busy now so I'm not bored, and his buddy Chet keeps a close eye on me, even though he tries to pass it off as just being friendly." She rolled her eyes. "We never talk about my past, and when I bring it up, he shuts down." She abandoned her spoon on the table and looked up, meeting Sebastian's return stare.

"What can I do to help?"

She fidgeted in her seat, looking uncomfortable. Nervous. "The funny thing is...I think you already are."

Sebastian laid his arm on the table across the front of him and leaned closer. "I'm sorry. I'm not following."

Kyra tilted her head back. The folds of her sage sweater flopped to the side, exposing the long gold necklace she wore. It slipped down over her white blouse. No hint of the tooth pendant Talia had told him to look for. Sebastian's jaw clenched, sending a tightened pain along the bone.

Kyra was frustrated, he could see that, but she didn't need to be. He was going to help her. When she looked at him again, her eyes sparked with what he took for determination. Her hand sprang forward, her fingers seeking his. Like a vine, her index finger twined around his, and her gaze melted into his return stare. "I don't know how to say this, so I'm just going to say it."

Sebastian glanced down at their hands, the way her pinkie wrapped around his, and a churn of warmth spread through his gut. Before seeing her, he'd begun to lose hope. Now pleasure, excitement, elation rushed him, tingled his senses, twitching and curving the edge of his lips to the heavens. Of course, he tried to play it off, mask it as an it's-all-cool grin. He looked back up to meet Kyra's gaze. "I'm good with that."

"I've been having dreams, and I think they're trying to tell me something. I think I'm trying to remember. In the dreams, it's always hot, and I'm always in distress, but every time you're there, and that gives me hope." Her fingers tightened on his. "Since that first day you showed up at my door, I've been determined to find you."

Sebastian knew exactly what memory she was describing. It made sense that if she remembered anything, she would remember that. It would have made a strong impression, a lasting memory. Purgatory was meant to dig deep into one's soul. The fact that she remembered him trying to save her... His chest was lighter than air. He could fly if he had to.

"Hey, Ky. I thought that looked like you."

Beside their table stood a medium-built guy. Dirty blond hair, brown eyes. Sebastian immediately disliked him. Maybe it was the way he placed his hand on Kyra's shoulder, or the way he shortened her name. He reminded Sebastian of Marcus. Kyra pulled her hand away from Sebastian and back into her lap.

"See you across the street in a few?" the guy asked.

Kyra twisted in her seat to take in the man standing at her side. "Good morning, Chet. It's nice to see you. Don't worry, I'll be there." She smiled, and it was the kind of smile you plastered on your face to show you had manners, when you really wanted nothing more than to be left alone. Sebastian was familiar with this look of hers. He held back a chuckle and watched her as the man continued to stand in silence at her side. With a sigh, she rolled her eyes at him. "I'll see you there, Chet." Her voice was short and decisive. No one could argue the message sent.

Chet lowered his head, making it impossible to see his expression. "Right. See you there. Watching the clock, Ky." He tapped his phone three times sharp, turned with an abrupt pivot, and walked away.

Sebastian sat back in his seat and stretched his legs out once again. "So...you go by Ky now?"

She shook her head. "It's just what Marcus and his friends call me." She looked at the time on her phone. Sebastian made note: she now carried a phone. No doubt so Marcus could get ahold of her whenever he wanted. "I have to get to work soon."

"Yeah, you have checking accounts to open and bills to count. Things like that?"

Kyra shot him a hurt scowl.

He felt the blow as if the car on the Kamikaze ride had slammed full force into his gut. "I'm sorry. That was a shit thing to say."

"I get it. I'm not the person you remember." She paused, glanced at her hands. "I want to remember who she was, I really do." She looked up, straight into his soul. "Will you meet me here again? Say, tomorrow morning?" Her hand wrapped around his once more, this time with more strength than she'd shown previously. It felt like a plea.

Tension tightened Sebastian's back and shoulders. It wasn't the request that got to him. It was the sound of her voice, the anxious need. "Better yet, why don't you ditch work? Come with me now. I can take you somewhere that might just be exactly what you need—" Without warning, Sebastian's jaw locked up, his every muscle froze, and he couldn't move. What the fuckin' hell is going on? his inner voice yelled, and his eyes darted left and right.

"Sebastian?" Kyra inquired. "You were saying?"

He couldn't respond. Couldn't will his mouth to work or voice to answer. But his gaze narrowed in on the culprit, standing not-so-inconspicuously by the creamer station. Tall, gray suit with hat pulled down to shield his facial features, and a cheesy name tag tacked to his chest, probably his father's lame idea. All part of the everyone-get-to-know-Sebastian movement. Except, all the names were fake. So what was the point? The Reaper across the room was no more named Mr. Johnson than his father was Mr. Smith.

Damn Reapers. Now Sebastian had a tail because his father didn't trust him on his own. His gaze shifted to Kyra.

"Sebastian?" Kyra's eyes bored into him, large and wide.

He knew the answer. Knew what it would take to escape the Reaper's grasp. His chest heaved, eyes closed, and he gave up the desire to whisk Kyra away. At least, for the moment. His father could have this one, but Sebastian would win in the end, Hell be damned.

The lock on his body released, sending him stumbling back into the cushion of his chair. Quick to recover, his hand raked through the hair across the top of his crown. "Sorry," he said. "Lost my thought."

"Tomorrow?" Kyra reminded him. "Can you meet me here?"

If the Reapers weren't going to let him have this moment with her, maybe he could get tomorrow. He discarded the cool act and let her see the raw side of himself. All the muscles in his face loosened as earnestness took up camp in his eyes. He sat up straight. "I can probably manage that."

"Only probably?"

He squeezed her hand back. "I'll be here, Kyra."

"Good." She stood to leave. Sebastian also stood. "Don't stand on my account."

"Don't be silly. I'll see you tomorrow then." Unsure of what to do, he held out his hand. She stared down at it for a second before taking it in her own. The shake felt awkward and out of place.

She turned to leave, paused, then spun around. Without warning, she threw herself forward, clasping her arms around his shoulders, pressing her soft body against his in a tight, warm hug. Even without her dragon, she burned like fire. Her heat embraced him, traveled through him, marrying them into one. All the time lost was forgotten. He didn't care about Marcus; she was with him now, in his arms where he'd always wanted her to be. He closed his eyes and buried his nose in her hair.

"You smell…" He paused, unsure of the word he wanted to use. "Different."

Kyra took a small step back. "I do?"

"Sunflowers," Sebastian said, tilting his head forward.

Understanding bloomed over her features. "You can smell them on me?"

"I can."

She bit her lip and her eyes sparkled, hinting to the wild gold they turned before she lost half herself. "I can't seem to get warm enough lately, so I've been filling the apartment with sunflowers to trick my mind. They are such a warm flower, don't you think?"

Sebastian nodded in agreement, but inwardly found her confession more than curious. Was she cold without her dragon to warm her?

Kyra looked around, then leaned into Sebastian once more. In his ear, she whispered, "Were we close?"

Her tone asked if they had been more than friends. He didn't know how to answer. He only knew how he had felt, and no longer knew how she had felt. Not after the kiss. The kiss loomed out there like an enormous unanswered question now that she didn't have her memory to tell him what it'd meant. From what he'd seen, she'd chosen Marcus over him. "I knew you well, but I only knew what you chose to share. As for close…I think you can answer that yourself, can't you? You are with Marcus, are you not?"

She stepped back, slowly letting her hand fall away. "Yes. Marcus." Her gaze lingered on Sebastian's. It burned a desire in him he feared no amount of reaping or lust fulfillment would ever quench. He wanted to know what thoughts ran through her head. The want built with fierce intensity into untethered need.

"Tomorrow, then." She walked from him straight out the door. Once on the street, she spared him a glance through the large picture window. He watched each step of her trek across the street until she disappeared into the bank.

"Infraction 183. Failure to comply with a superior Grim." Mr. Johnson stood at Sebastian's side. "This is your first warning. You only get—"

"Yeah, yeah, I know." Sebastian sat with such force the chair scooted a few inches across the floor. He didn't care what Mr. Johnson had to say. Kyra, here. And now tomorrow. His mind buzzed with new thoughts and images. Possibilities. She had opened up new prospects. Prospects he was eager to explore.

He downed his coffee and smashed the cup flat on the table. Adrenaline pumped through his veins like the Four Horsemen racing into the Apocalypse. He stood and turned toward the nearest trashcan. Mr. Johnson was gone, his job done, the warning delivered. But something else at the front of the shop flashed, catching his attention. All too quickly it vanished.

What had he seen? He pushed at the tiny memory, hand pressed to the side of his skull. Someone had been watching him from the front window. Dropping his trash on the table, Sebastian bolted for the front of the shop. The street beyond was alive with the usual morning hustle. Cars zipped this way and that. People moved along the sidewalks with purpose, shops and businesses their likely destinations. Nothing looked out of the ordinary, yet his penetrating gaze searched all directions and came up empty. Maybe he was being paranoid. Maybe he had imagined the whole thing.

He pushed the suspicion from his mind and headed down the street toward Sophie's parents' place. Walked past shops and businesses to the narrow alleyway with a side door into their apartment building. Tall buildings on either side pressed in, trying to reclaim the ground, creating a dark and tight squeeze of a space. A single sound bounced off the stark brick walls confining the area. So narrow was the passage and so tall the sidewalls that little to no sunlight reached the asphalt. Not that it was dark enough to worry about losing one's way, only dark enough to hide distinguishing features.

An old, emerald Impala was now parked in the path, and the building's side door sat slightly ajar. There was no evidence of people nearby—no voices or conversations lingered in the air— yet Sebastian received a steady stream of memories. Thoughts and memories that made little to no sense to him. Were the owners all soon to be among the dead? If so, where were they? That was how Sebastian's gift usually worked. The dead and near-dead, whether they knew it or not, transmitted their thoughts and memories like a homing beacon for Reapers.

Sebastian stood at the entrance of the alley, perfectly still, alert, attuned to every click and scuff and echo bouncing off the cold, hard stone.

"Sebastian."

His name slithered along the cracks in the block walls, across the paved ground, unfurling like the tongue of a reptilian predator. Sebastian straightened and tilted his head to the sound, following the echo as it moved through the arena. Because that's what he saw this soon becoming—a field of combat. Three steps into the alley, the sound changed, morphed, became haunting. Hauntingly beautiful.

"I know you're here. Show yourself," Sebastian called out. He continued to move deeper into the tight space, closer to the apartment building's entrance. Muscles taut and jaw rigid, he prepared for what lay in wait. He considered himself ready for anything. The inner buzz from one of his mother's kind was unexpected. He'd not been in the presence of a Mara since his mother had abandoned him as a child. He'd been left alone to stumble through his learning, and despised her for it. Despised his Mara half. Besides, Maras were not to be trusted. "Mother?" he whispered, taking another step into the shadows.

The car was hidden in the dark, a few feet up ahead. It rattled and creaked, bouncing twice on its hind springs. Expecting to find his mother working her sorcery on some willing schmuck in the backseat, Sebastian approached with caution. He peered through the Impala's side window. No one was inside. The car was empty. Any hint reminding him of his mother was gone. But something else caught his attention: movement around the front edge, near the headlight. A shuffle and scamper unlike the grace of any Mara. The muscle at the side of his eye twitched. Somebody was playing games, and he had never been one for games.

Mr. Johnson stood near the entrance of the alleyway, his silhouette highlighted by the light of day bright on the street beyond. He whipped out a notepad and started taking notes.

Hell's fire! Damn Reapers, thought Sebastian. Is this a test?

Metal groaned and a green block popped up in his peripheral view. It was the Impala's trunk lid pointing to the sky. From the open space spilled a couple of quick, dark figures. Sebastian tensed, then threw his arms out defensively. Whatever they were, they had him flanked. He glanced at the building entrance. Could he make it without a fight? Did he even want to? Any kind of weapon would come in handy about now. Even one of those sickles he'd seen in so many silly images portraying Reapers.

He darted for the door. A blur shot straight at him, and pain splintered through his ribs. He felt the blow before he saw the crowbar. Fire spread through his side, sharp at the center and dulling as it spread outward. Ignoring instinct telling him to protect his ribs, Sebastian moved forward, pushing into the attackers.

Something caught him before he saw it, the weight knocking him to the ground. Metal netting had been dumped over the top of him. Everywhere the binding touched his skin stung, the links reeking of a bittersweet aroma. He scrunched his nose to block out the smell. It reminded him of caramel syrup, too sugary. He felt dizzy and the images before him swayed. It wasn't going to stop him, though. He shoved up off the asphalt, dragging the heavy curtain draped over him. Muscles ached in ways they never had before. Sebastian stumbled and fell into one of his attackers. A man blending in with the shadows.

A snort came from behind.

More hoots and chortles from the rear. Whoever they were, they had cast the net over him. Snuck up on him while he'd been engaged with the two who'd jumped out of the trunk— decoys.

"Can you believe this guy?" someone at his right said. "Look at him still fighting. Even wrapped in the Mara Web."

The what? No!

Sebastian tried to steady his breath, even as his heart attempted to hammer its way through his chest. He didn't believe it. Mara Webs didn't exist. They were a myth created to make humans feel better. Feel safe from the nightmare of monsters.

He struggled. With each move he made, the net tightened, hugged closer to his body. It wasn't a myth. He could feel the net working, turning his own power against him. It plucked his nightmares from his head and played them back, remaking his reality. Only he knew better. He knew he was still struggling in metal mesh, on the ground of a tight, dark alley. He knew the pictures he saw of himself, of Kyra, were only an illusion and nothing more.

And yet, they didn't keep him from struggling. He didn't want to see. Wasn't sure he could stomach his worst nightmares. And the more he struggled, the more he felt his life force drain from his body. Could he die? He'd never asked that question of his father. Right now he really wanted to know.

Slowly, methodically, his hands reached out for the edge of the net. It took all his concentration and it felt like an eternity to accomplish the task. Sweat trickled down his temple and he was instantly on the boardwalk watching Chow Lien paint—the moment he had learned to harness his inner strength, use it as a shield. That was what he needed to do now. Needed to stay on point, to remember. His hands wrapped around the chain's edge and began to lift.

"You see that?" A voice on his left.

Sebastian felt a blunt hit to the shoulder blade and he wavered. His eyes fluttered shut, open, shut, then open again.

He collapsed to a sitting position. Watched their feet gather around him. There were five of them. It was embarrassing, a Reaper taken down by five lesser beings. Be them demon or men, he did not know. Although he didn't really care much now.

Sebastian turned his face up to his captors. It was hard to discern between the truth and the images placed in his mind by the net, but what he thought he saw were demons disguised as men. They had to be Marcus's men. Demons and Marcus, seemed like a logical association. "I let her be. What more does Marcus want from me?" he bellowed, and felt his body burn with emotion he couldn't express.

One set of boots stepped closer. Close enough to see the scuff across the center of the right tip, and the threads were starting to show. "Think you got it all wrong, bud," the owner of the boots said and kicked Sebastian hard to the gut. It felt like a sledgehammer wielded by the carnival's strongman. Sebastian coughed, splattering blood across the cracked asphalt. "I." He kicked Sebastian again. "Honestly." And again. "Don't." And again. "Care." Then he leaned down, closer to Sebastian's eye level. "None of us care what you did or didn't do. Thing is, Boss wants you. That means I gotta bag ya."

Sebastian's glance darted to where Mr. Johnson had been. The Reaper was no longer there. In fact, he was nowhere. He was gone. This probably wasn't a test. It was too brutal.

The guy bent down, got right in Sebastian's face. His eyes were dark pools of ink. They matched the midnight matted hair that lay across his head and hinted to the beast hidden beneath the human mask. His teeth were sharp nails.

Sebastian studied him, tried to identify his species, but all he really wanted to do was sleep. His eyelids felt heavy. Letting his captors win actually seemed like a plausible choice.

"So, this boss of yours?" Sebastian prompted.

The guy poked him hard in the shoulder with his index finger. It knocked Sebastian off balance, toppling him all the way to the ground. All the bodies gathered around him laughed. Sebastian lifted himself partway up.

"She's going to take pleasure tearing you apart." His eyes sparked, and he rubbed his fingers together enthusiastically. "And I will take great pleasure in tenderizing you." His fist slammed into Sebastian's face.

Everything turned the most brilliant color of white. Sebastian imagined this must be what it looked like for his clients moving through the doorway onto the other side. So fantastical.

Then his head hit the ground.

He was drained and exhausted. Rest sounded like a good idea. Only for a few minutes. Then he'd have his strength back, and he'd bring down Hell's fury on these little brimstone shitters.

Closing his eyes, he forgot his cares and the real, unjust world. He let the Mara within him pick his future. Eyes closed, he drifted off to sleep.

He was only mildly aware when they shoved him in a trunk with the net still wrapped around him, and hauled him out sometime later.

EARLY

The coffee needed to be stronger. Much stronger. What it really needed was a shot of the good stuff. Marcus opened the cabinet above the bar and grabbed a bottle of his private stock. Without a word to his houseguest, he poured a shot in the mug in front of him and took a sip. Better, but he wasn't there yet. He closed his eyes and rolled his head and shoulders. Way too much tension. His rotator cuff tendons popped.

"Tell me again," he said. "Why is he down at the club?"

Leila stood in the middle of the kitchen, still as a statue, her robes draping onto the floor like an old painter's cloth. "Because, old friend, I have use for the boy."

Marcus huffed. He wasn't pleased with the way things were going, but he wasn't ready to sever his relationship with Leila just yet. She was still useful. "Make sure you keep him out of my way. I don't want him meddling in any more of my plans."

Leila had her arms folded across the front of her, and the sleeves of her cloak covered every bit of her form, dripping down the front of her like melted wax. She opened her arms wide, breaking the impression, and feigned a small curtsy. Marcus knew it to be bullshit. Stubborn as she was, she bowed to no one. "Of course, my lord. Your agenda is the priority above all."

"If that's the case, why not simply cut his throat? He's unnecessary baggage." Marcus took a slow sip of his coffee and watched Leila over the rim of his mug.

She lurched forward, slamming her hands on the counter. "He

is mine! Understand? You don't harm him unless I say so." Her voice seethed with rivaling authority, and yet she spoke so softly Marcus found himself leaning closer.

There was no sweat or flinch on Marcus's end. His reaction was to laugh. Except, he knew laughter wouldn't serve his purpose. It would only upset the wild spirit standing in his kitchen, and he needed all his pawns in line.

"Very well, Leila. I'll play it your way—for now." He set his coffee on the counter. "But consider this a warning. If I find him, at any point, standing between me and what I want, I will not hesitate."

Leila's eyes glowed from beneath her hood. The effect diminished her pretty face. For the briefest of moments, Marcus tried to imagine what it would be like to be one of her conquests. Were the days so unbelievable, the sex so astonishing, that the nightmares were overlooked? The slow drain of life left unnoticed? He found it hard to believe.

The front door banged shut. Marcus spun around to see Kyra standing there with keys in hand, a stunned look etched on her face. Her burgundy handbag flopped from her shoulder to the crook of her arm. She didn't move. "I didn't expect…"

"Got home early." Marcus leaned against the counter dividing the small living area from the kitchen. As he did, he casually glanced back into the little room. Leila was gone, the sliding door to the balcony open. "You too, I see."

Kyra moved into the room. She set her purse and keys on the coffee table. "I was feeling a bit off. Decided to come home."

Marcus raked his eyes over her from head to toe. He could tell she was acting different, even if she tried to hide it. He suspected it had to do with her morning encounter. Even if she wouldn't readily divulge any information, he knew everything that went on in her life. He left nothing to chance. Negating the space between them, he wrapped her in his arms and kissed her tenderly on the forehead. "You alright? Need to rest?"

She turned away from him and laid the back of her head on his shoulder. The aversion didn't go unnoticed—the fact she made no immediate attempt to circle her arms around his waist. More often than not these days, her embrace was far too loose. He was losing her. He wanted to blame that little carnie fuck for showing up this morning, but he knew the truth. He'd been losing her for a while.

Didn't matter. Once he got his dragon back, she would fall in love with him. Women loved power. He would be the epitome of power. All beasts within the heavens, on earth, and in the underworld would bow to him. For he was, and would be again, the most feared dragon of them all. Fire raced through his veins, laced with the laughter of his oncoming victory. He would rule once again. Rule it all.

He looked down at Kyra. "I will take you for my queen."

She blinked and the edges of her eyes crinkled as her face torqued. "What?"

Marcus didn't answer. Not with words. He turned her to face him and pressed his lips to hers, hard and furious. His hand dragged through the locks at the back of her head while the other pulled her in tighter and lifted her off the ground. She was his and no other's. He would mark her as so.

CAGED

Blood dribbled down Sebastian's chin, staining the front of his shirt. Liquid copper filled his mouth. He spat the blood clear, but its flavor lingered, seeping around his teeth and gums.

The Mara Web was gone and he sat chained to a chair in the center of a large cage. The space was the size of a tiny bedroom, barely enough height for him to stand on his toes and stretch his arms above his head. As things stood, he wasn't moving from the spot. He'd given up struggling against the bonds hours ago.

The room containing his prison gave little clue to where he was. No sound from the outside world reached its way in. He took that to mean the walls were heavily insulated. The souls in the surrounding area hinted to a commercial setting. As did the memories of his captor. Memories—now they were an interesting reveal. Be it tomorrow or next month, the fact Sebastian could pick the memories from the air meant the monster in front of him had already been scheduled for demise. Sebastian had felt the same mortality in the alleyway, earlier. Although, there were more memories then, from more monsters.

Whack!

The hit was hard, solid, and Sebastian's head swung to the side with the force of the blow. The stocky guard grinned before hitting Sebastian in the jaw again.

Sebastian spat more blood onto the prison floor. "Is there a point to this? An interrogation, perhaps?"

The guard rocked back on his heels. "Nah. Just like it." He stood towering over Sebastian, filling all available space from the floor to the top of his cage.

"Excellent." Sebastian's word dripped with sarcasm.

The door at the far side of the room opened, the thick metal dragging across the cement ground with a scraauch. Light shifted and spilled in from the opening, and three people entered. More toy soldiers, Sebastian thought. Two took a seat at the table in the corner, ignoring Sebastian and his tormentor, but one made eye contact. He leaned against the edge of the bars, scrutinized the beating Sebastian received. Based on the guy's speckled gray hair, Sebastian guessed he was the oldest in the room. Then again, maybe not. It was only a mask, after all. All his captors had remained camouflaged in human form. For his benefit, he suspected.

"You've done enough, Dover." Stepping into the cage, the older guy dropped his hand on Dover's shoulder. "Leave some for me. Others like to have fun, too."

Dover's face morphed into a sure-thing sneer, as much as the monster-man could sneer, and in that moment, Sebastian saw the gray, wrinkled skin and horned nose. He narrowed his stare at his beast of a captor. "Absolutely, Boss," Dover grumbled, then spit at Sebastian and stepped aside, taking up residence in the far corner of the confined space. Sebastian ignored the gesture. Instead, he focused his attention on the new boss in the room taking point.

"If the purpose of all this is to annoy me, you're doing a damn good job," Sebastian said.

Boss laughed and dragged a chair into the space. Spinning the back to Sebastian, he sat straddling the seat and set his gaze on his captive. The seconds ticked by without a word. The sound of his steady breath imitated a metronome, not that Sebastian needed any relaxation triggers. He was fine. "You seem to be quite the prize. People want you something awful," Boss said.

Sebastian noted Boss was rather stout, most likely an aspect of his true being. Sebastian tilted his head, feigning sincere interest. "By people, you mean…?"

Boss pointed. "That's not going to work. You won't get any

information out of me, nightmare creature. So tell me—thing—
what does it feel like to be the only boy in an all-girls club?"

Sebastian raised a brow. He picked up on the subtleties. Boss
was talking about his Mara nature. There was no mention of
Sebastian's other ability. He was beginning to think the Mara in
him was all they cared about. Maybe it was all they knew about.
He wondered how he could use that narrow knowledge to his
advantage. He shifted in his tight position, tried to get comfortable and look laid-back, indifferent. He didn't want these guys to
think he was intimidated. "It's kinda cool, actually. Who wouldn't
want to be the only guy? The ladies adore me." Sebastian tossed
his head back and gave what he thought might be a cocky grin.

Dover dashed across the cage and slammed him in the face,
a head-butt—face to face. It was like getting smashed with a skull
of iron.

Sebastian grimaced. Tried to pinch away the blinding light of
fracturing pain. "Hey! Can you keep your dino off me?"

The room filled with low laughter. Boss looked to the group,
then assessed Dover, before returning his attention to Sebastian.
"No, I don't think I will." He laid his arms across the back of the
chair and leaned closer. "You see, that's not how things are going
to work. You might be used to being something special," he used
air quotes for emphasis, "worthy of VIP treatment, but you're
not. On the contrary, you're a freak. You never should have been.
Maras are like banshees, a role meant to be filled by women. So
tell me, why you?" He cradled his chin in his hand and waited for
Sebastian's answer.

Sebastian spat more blood. He wanted to wipe his lip, but
knew any effort to do so was a waste of time. A heavy sigh heaved
through his chest. "I don't know. Why is anything the way it is?"

"You're an anomaly. A monstrosity. Her reason for wanting
you is incomprehensible." Boss turned to his comrades in the
room. "Right, guys?" They roared in concurrence.

"Who?" Sebastian questioned. "Was it the Mara I felt in
the alley?"

Boss didn't answer. Instead, he stood, pushed the chair away, and began to pace within the cage's small confines. The keys clipped to his belt jingled at his hip and his fingers clutched nervously at the side of his gun, never actually touching the metal. His other hand scratched at his hair. "What I don't get, and maybe you can explain this to me"—the gun came free of its holster and he began to wave it in slow swirls—"is for a monster, Maras are too damn beautiful. I mean, demon-damn-dazzling. It ain't right. Look at you!"

Maybe he was about to die at Boss's pent-up anger and frustration. Didn't matter. Sebastian couldn't stop himself from grinning. Emotion such as Boss's was always personal. Considering what Boss was doing to him, Sebastian didn't feel too sorry for any misery some Mara had caused him or his family in the past.

"You got a name?" Sebastian asked.

Boss turned the gun on Sebastian and aimed it between his eyes. "What the demon hell does my name have to do with anything?"

"Only trying to be civil. Don't want to share, that's fine. I'll call you Boss-boy. How does that sound?"

Boss-boy growl-grunted at Sebastian's insult of a name and pushed the gun up through his hair.

Sebastian remained steady, knowing any wrong move risked setting Boss-boy off in a terrible way. "Let me explain something I've come to understand about Maras." Sebastian watched Boss-boy as he moved across the back of the cage, and then returned to the chair propped in front of him. Boss-boy watched him through squinted eyes and harnessed his gun. Sebastian took his cue. "A Mara's true face is anything but beautiful. You only see beauty because your brain cannot interpret the truth. It is easily fooled by the harmonics at which she resonates. It causes your brain to perceive her as magnificent. The reality is far different. Kind of like you folks." Sebastian turned his head and spit blood residue in the direction of their audience. "We all know you don't look like this in your true form, do you?"

Dover laughed. Not Boss-boy, though. He snarled and his face shifted to a beast form, flesh pulled tight over his skull in long bands. Finally, a pure view. Sebastian immediately recognized him as a behemoth. The two at the table looked in their direction and for a second Sebastian could see their true faces, as well. Everyone in the room was a behemoth.

That couldn't be good. A room full of chaos monsters the size of hippos. Someone had it out for him.

"What purpose do you guys stand to gain holding me?" Sebastian asked.

"I don't like him." The call came from the table in the corner. Sebastian strained to see which of the two had spoken. It was unclear.

Dover's hand twisted on the bars of the cage, his gaze burning into Sebastian. Sebastian was confident that if it were up to that man, he'd already be dead. He wasn't sure what he'd done to deserve it, but pure hatred boiled in Dover's irises. The guy's festering emotions ate away at Sebastian's Reaper intake channels.

Boss-boy sat sideways on the chair. He rocked back and forth, carving a small hole in the seat with his knife. "Just keeping you out of the way. That's all we got to do. Keep you out of the way."

Things were clicking into place for Sebastian. He suddenly feared for Kyra more than ever. "What are you talking about?"

The behemoth snapped his head and stared at Sebastian. His eyes were stained with a multitude of blood-colored cracks. "Nothing."

Dover stepped forward. "Boss?" His head jerked back around. "His Majesty didn't say anything about keeping him alive. Only the Mara did. Since when do we take orders from her?"

"Damn straight!" Boss-boy said. The behemoths shook their heads. "But he is listening to her." Boss-boy stared into the space of the cell.

Sebastian glanced between them, soaking in their words and appraising their mental states. There was a Mara in the mix, working with Marcus, and for whatever reason, she wanted Sebastian. How could he use that information to his advantage? "Tell you what. Why don't you at least loosen these chains, so my limbs don't fall off? How 'bout we start there?" Sebastian spoke quietly.

Every sound bounced off the room's walls, magnifying tenfold.

"Why don't you shut the freak up!" Dover yelled.

Sebastian went silent and watched him.

"What the hell you looking at? You think I'm funny-looking? A little too fat, too big? Can't hold a candle to a pretty Mara boy?" His hand twisted on the cage. The metal groaned and tore. He now held a long, jagged shaft like a weapon.

"Hey." Sebastian stumbled for words. "I think you need to calm down."

Boss-boy stood, moved the chair out of the way. "I probably should have told you. His dad was sucked dry by a Mara. He has a bit of a problem with your kind."

Sebastian's eyes grew wide as he watched Dover retreat and join the others at the table. Where was his father when he could actually use the bastard? Damnation. He didn't want to go out this way. Not before he saved Kyra from her plight.

Sebastian cleared his throat and addressed Dover. "Sorry about your father. You know I had nothing to do with that, right? I don't hunt like a Mara. You've got me all wrong." Dover's hand tightened on the metal rod and beads of sweat ran down the side of his face.

From the far end of the room, beyond the closed door, pops exploded. Shots were being fired. Confusion flashed across Dover's face. It turned to resignation and he moved back toward the cell with purpose. Is someone finally coming to help me? Sebastian wondered. Maybe. Or maybe it was something else entirely, and he was going to get caught in the crossfire.

Everyone in the room was on the move: Boss-boy on Dover's heels, the others running for the door. "They're coming. Secure the room," Boss yelled.

Sebastian looked around wildly. Looked at their faces, then to the door. "Who's coming?"

More shots rang out. Yells and screams echoed through the wall. A banging on the heavy metal of the secured door followed. Something was trying to break into his prison room.

"I'm here!" Sebastian called out.

"Shut up, you freak!" Dover shoved the steel rod through Sebastian's stomach.

Sebastian's mouth slumped open and he looked at the metal protruding from his body. Blood spilled out at an alarming rate. Dover stood before him with a wicked grin on his face. Sebastian wanted to knock the irritating look off, but his hands were still tied and his strength was draining fast. He whispered, strained and difficult, blood sputtering from his lips.

Dover leaned forward. Sebastian saw Boss-boy behind him, not disapproving of the turn in events. "What was that?" Dover teased.

Sebastian pulled deep from his core, looking for his voice. Dark, slithering power came up in a graveled gnarl, vibrating his ribs and vocal cords. The room resonated with rage and agony as the growl shifted into a scream. A pitch-black sound, through and through.

Dover stepped back, stumbling on air. "He's a Rea—" Blood streamed from his eyes and he fell to the ground.

Boss-boy grabbed his head, pressed into the sides, and screamed. Everyone withered. Howling, bleeding, dying. The room shifted. Moved in and out of shape. Sounds muffled. And Sebastian's breath labored. He lowered his head. Strength waned, and the chains still held him to the chair. His body slumped against them.

What have I done? Sebastian's mind stammered. How?

Footsteps. So many of them rushing into the room. A hand lifted his head and a face came right up to his. The small beam of a flashlight zipped back and forth across his eyes. "He's in bad shape, sir," the person said. He lowered Sebastian's head slowly.

Someone tugged at the steel bar in his stomach. Sebastian screamed. White-hot lights flashed through his body.

"Get him unshackled," someone said.

People began to tug and pull at him. Excruciating—he tried to yell. The pain was both dull and sharp at different points. A young girl dropped at his side. She pushed his hair back from his face. Drenched with sweat, it stuck to the side of his brow. "You'll be alright. I promise," she said.

Sebastian blinked. Then she yanked the rod from his body. He was doused in Kyra's fire, plummeting into the screaming pits of Hell, and everything went black.

5

DRAGONS

Sparks swirled like a hostile whirlwind within the glass jar. Marcus studied it a moment, then set the jar in the passenger seat of his Mustang. His fingers drummed on the dashboard and he gazed out the front windshield at the vivid colors of the day. The cheerful birdsong in the trees, the bright sun illuminating everything in brilliance. None of it meant anything to him. All his concern was wrapped up in what the contents of the glass jar beside him represented. Was this the combination he wanted? He had to be sure. After a long pause, he picked up his phone and dialed the number he'd come to know so well. It rang only once.

"I'm ready," he said. "Let's do this thing." He listened to the voice on the other end and a discontented frown began to form on his face. "Why not tonight?" He paused. "Yes, I want to do it right!" A streak of frustration flashed through him. "Alright then, we'll do it your way. You'd better be there."

He ended the call and glanced down at the jar. The dragon within clawed at the glass. They all did that. Never content in their temporary confinement. Just as well. Marcus didn't want complacent beasts. Not for this ritual.

Turning the key and roaring the engine to life, he shifted into gear and rolled back onto the street. He would take the newly acquired forest beast and add her to the others. Trees and bushes blurred past. The bridge. The same bridge where he had met Kyra. Now there was a special find. He'd lucked out finding her. If only he could pinpoint all the dragons in the same state as her—products of two different breeding lines, leaving her trapped in-between and young enough to still make a choice. He'd gotten two for the price of one with Kyra. Her dragon could morph either way. Such a treasure.

He glanced back down at the jar in the next seat. Not that beastie, though. Today's catch was an ordinary Forest Dragon. A relatively easy catch. Practically rolled over and begged him to take her. Oh, the things he'd done to her. His lips curled up and the tip of his tongue explored the edges of his teeth in a deliciously slow move.

At the corner stop sign, he moved out of the civic park and into the traffic of the city. His condo was fifteen minutes away, a little more if traffic got heavy. Glancing around at the cars pushing their way down the street, and then at the jar sitting on the seat beside him, an idea bloomed. He reached over into the back and grabbed the jacket he'd left there on a previous night, draped it over the dragon's prison, hiding it from view. He detected the tiniest of objections—a small roar—but knew the beast was securely trapped within the confined space. Safe from discovery. For now.

Twenty minutes later, Marcus pulled up in front of his condo. Carrying the magical dragon wrapped in his jacket, he locked the car and walked across the parking complex to the stairs. His condo was on the second level. He'd ascended halfway when his phone rang.

Pulling his phone from his pocket, he checked the screen before answering. His club. Tension was building in his jaw and neck before he pushed the button and put the phone to his ear, a bad feeling brewing in his gut. A voice on the other end immediately broke into bluster.

"What do you mean, he's gone?" Marcus listened and his body tensed, filling with heat. "How are they dead?" He paused. "That doesn't make sense." Marcus moved the phone from his face and yelled to the sky, then returned to the conversation. "Don't touch anything in that room. I'll be there as soon as I can."

Hanging up and shoving the phone in the breast pocket of his suit jacket, he dashed up the remaining steps quick as he could.

Last thing he needed was the damn carnie on the loose. Kyra had left early to wait for the irritating carnie punk at the coffee shop that morning. She'd made up some lame excuse about work, but Marcus knew the truth. He had informants, and Chet was keeping a close eye on her. That's how he knew she'd held out until the last possible moment before abandoning the wait and checking into work. She'd also spent her break at the stupid shop. Marcus didn't want the boy to show up now, swoop in and act the big hero, mess up all his plans.

Marcus entered his condo and rushed from room to room to verify he was alone. Satisfied he was the only one present, he moved to his secret hiding place on the balcony. When he was sure no one was watching, he shoved the Forest Dragon into place with the others. The addition made a total of five liberated dragons. Five dragons he would make his own. Marcus smiled, then slammed the front of the secret passage shut.

Now for Kyra. She'd be so much more valuable at my side if she had her dragon, he thought. Plus, I'd be able to control her better. Problem was, he wanted her dragon more than any other. Maybe he would get her a different dragon. A smaller, more docile beast. One more appropriate for his concubine.

He pushed off the wall and rushed back out toward his car. He had to get to her before the idiot carnie did. Who knew what he was up to? Blast that Sebastian.

Twenty-five minutes later, Marcus pulled into the bank parking lot to a cast of chaos. Red lights were spinning, cop cars blocked the entrance, and people wandered about in varied levels of excitement and fear.

His mind flew to the worst place first. Bank robbery. He was sure of it. How many banks were robbed in a day? He'd have to look up the statistics. He had foolishly let Kyra work at a financial institution. His jaw grew taut and he shoved looky-loos and bank employees out of his path, making his way for the front door.

Chet grabbed his arm. "Hey man. A bank robbery. Can you believe it?" He took a long drag on his cigarette. "Caught the jackals, though." He pointed to a police car parked a few yards away, using his hand with the cigarette pinched between his fingers. Two people sat in the back. "They looked ordinary enough."

Marcus adjusted his sunglasses to better see the suspects. "What is that, a husband and wife team? They could be anyone. They don't look at all threatening."

"I think that was the point. Made it all the way to the counter. No one suspected. They looked so normal. It wasn't until Bethany panicked that we knew something was going down. If she had simply handed over the money, they probably would have walked out and no one would have been the wiser. But she freaked and started crying. The gal next to her knew something was up. It just snowballed from there." Chet took another drag from his cigarette, shifted his feet, and shoved his free hand in his pocket. "The wifey perp, she pressed the demands on Bethany, and at that point the husband whipped out the gun. It could have gotten real ugly, and it was pretty scary for a few minutes there, let me tell ya. But your gal—wow!"

Marcus's jaw clenched. "Kyra? What did she do?"

Chet clamped his hands on Marcus's upper arms. "She saved the day, man! She saved everyone."

Marcus knocked Chet's hands free and stormed toward the bank. He could feel the steam pouring off his skull. A policeman's arm shot out in front of him. "I'm sorry, sir. The bank is closed."

Marcus looked around the man, searching everything and everyone in sight. He spotted Kyra talking with another officer and pointed. "I'm here for her. She's my fiancée."

The officer looked over his shoulder at Kyra, made eye contact with the agent interviewing her, and then waved Marcus through. The doors to the bank were propped open. A patch of smeared blood at about waist height marked where someone had slammed into the exit far too hard. He recalled the male suspect holding an icepack on his head.

Kyra stood and moved across the room to meet him. "Bit of excitement today," she said with a tentative smile.

He walked around her, his gaze searching for anything amiss. "I can see that."

She turned, tried to follow him. "What are you doing?"

"Just making sure you're alright. I heard you were playing hero. That's dangerous, Kyra. When people do dangerous things, they tend to get hurt."

Kyra placed her hands on her hips and tilted her head to the side. Her red curls bounced with her stubborn poise. "I'm fine. You needn't worry about me."

He stopped and took a deep breath. His gaze fell on her cold, deep-set eyes. "This time, but what about the next? When are you going to stop playing hero?" Kyra jerked back. Marcus realized his mistake too late. She was smart, caught it immediately. That was one of the things he liked about her. It was also one of the things he found most infuriating. "How will I have you around forever if you choose to do foolhardy things like attack bank robbers?"

"Is that what you think? When have I played hero before? This, here." She gestured to the teller's window. "This was easy. I saw the whole thing in my head before I made a single move. I knew I could do it. If I hadn't known, I wouldn't have done it."

Marcus squinted. That made things worse. She was regaining her confidence. Soon he would lose her to the powerful being she was before, with or without her dragon. He moved in close until his cheek was against hers. Her breath warmed his skin and he breathed in the scent of her with each and every inhale. Slowly he wrapped his arms around her. Her body trembled. It was excellent he could still make her tremble.

His hand threaded through her hair, yanked her head back, exposing her neck. As he skimmed the soft curve with his kiss, a gentle moan of pleasure escaped her lips. Lips he would soon tease with his own.

She pushed him back. "Not here."

His grip tightened. "Never do such a foolish thing again. Understand?"

Kyra shuddered and shoved Marcus away. He grabbed her by the wrist and led her toward the car.

A police officer stepped in their path. "I'm sorry, ma'am. We aren't quite finished yet."

Kyra stopped and threw her hand to her chest. "Oh. So sorry. Of course." She turned to Marcus. "I shouldn't be much longer."

Marcus nodded and watched her return with the officer to the bank. He waited, stiff and stern, with his arms crossed. Chet came and stood at his side. Without looking at his friend, Marcus began to talk. "The blasted carnie boy escaped. I want him found, and I want Kyra watched even more closely until it is done."

"Got it," Chet said. He dropped his cigarette and ground it out with the bottom of his shoe. "I could take Kyra out tonight. Keep her occupied so she isn't looking for the kid. I'll take her to the circus she keeps asking about. She'd love that."

Marcus's ears started turning red and he turned to look at Chet. "That is the most idiotic idea I've heard yet. The circus? Seriously, Chet? Get your fucking act together or I'll have to cut you loose!"

Chet gulped. "Sorry, Boss. Wasn't thinking." He returned his gaze to the bank.

"That's for damn sure." Marcus stared at the bank and wondered what the next few days would bring. What the future with Kyra would bring. And what it would feel like to sink his teeth into Sebastian's skin, ripping him into dragon dinner scraps. The mere vision had him salivating at the chops.

6

ALICE

White light bled through the peace of the dark marsh behind Sebastian's closed eyes. He shifted, moved away from the annoyance. Hellfire exploded across his side and abdomen. He was being torn apart. Human shish kebab wasn't something he ever wanted to experience again. He groaned and his body moved, paused, and shifted some more, attempting to find a comfortable position. It wasn't happening.

His eyes fluttered, opened like slits. If the smell was any indication of what he would find, nothing good awaited. Wherever he was, it was rotten. He expected to find himself deep within the sewer system, among filth and waste. All he saw were dark, stark walls. He was lying stomach down on a mattress, though, and that had to count for something. Not the most comfortable mattress, nor the cleanest mattress he'd ever been on, but a bed all the same.

A cold, damp weight pressed against the back of his neck, and his body went rigid.

"Don't be alarmed. You're safe now. I'll see to it that you get all better."

The voice was female. He remembered a woman right before he'd blacked out. She'd been with the group who had stormed into his prison cell. She'd pulled the rod from his abdomen. In slow, methodical moves, he twisted, shifting to see her better. Every movement throbbed with torture. With clenched teeth, he held back the erupting madness. When he'd positioned himself away from the wall and faced her, he stopped, gently easing into place. His eyes closed to the burn flooding his system. Like lava rushing out around the wound. "Where am I?" he whispered.

She moved the compress to his forehead. "Somewhere safe. Do you have any idea what Balidhug's people wanted with you?"

Sebastian opened his eyes and gazed upon her for the first time with a steady eye. "By Balidhug, do you mean Marcus? He was the one behind it all, wasn't he?" Her lips twisted to the side. It was a look of unknowing. He reached out his hand and laid it upon hers. When he did so, he saw the crisscrossing bruises of the Mara Web pattern across the back of his hand. "It's alright if you don't know."

"I'm sorry. I only know what Davies tells me. Nothing more." She pulled her hand away and plucked at her bangs, straightening them over her forehead. Her dirty blonde hair was pulled back tight into a pony and she had on little to no makeup. There was a vague familiarity about the girl, but Sebastian couldn't quite place the feeling. Maybe it was the loose, comfortable fatigues in which she was wrapped. Army beige. A wannabe soldier. The thought jumped into Sebastian's mind because she looked the part, but lacked the heart. That was the sense he picked up from her. Interesting that was all he picked up from her or the surrounding space, and due to simple observation. Not by means of any supernatural gifts. He searched inward. Had his injury dulled or nullified his abilities?

"Who's Davies?" he asked.

She didn't look him in the eye. She continued to wipe at his skin with the cloth. It tingled and sent an odd sensation through his body. About the time it began to feel rough against his skin, she would retrieve a bottle from the floor and douse it with more ointment. The only word on the label was healer. He would have preferred a bit more information. Some ingredients, perhaps. "Davies is our crew leader. He thinks since Balidhug's people wanted you, you could be useful in the fight against them."

Sebastian grinned, painfully so. He was a pawn, and both sides wanted to use him. But to what end? "What's your name?"

Her eyes flickered up and her hand fumbled. She slipped a little too close to the bandaged hole in the side of Sebastian's abdomen. He winced and his fingers clenched. Her hands flew to his chest, as if by touching him she could suck the pain away. "I'm sorry. So sorry."

"Forget it." Sebastian spoke between gritted teeth. "You didn't mean to. Name?"

She pulled back. "Sorry. I'm Alice."

"Well, Alice, I'm not sure what help I can be. I think I got grabbed mostly to be kept out of the way."

"Ah, but don't you see? If he wants you out of the way, that means you are a threat to him. So yes, you can be of help." She stood from her place on the side of the bed. "I should tell Davies you are awake now."

Sebastian slid his hand off the bed and reached to stop her. "Alice?" She paused at his side and looked down. He lifted the bottle from the floor. "What is this stuff?"

"Is it making you feel strange?"

"It does stir an odd sensation, and this label isn't very revealing."

Her lips lifted at the corners and she reached down to take the bottle from him. She studied the worn typeset on the small white sticker before setting it back on the floor, this time at the head of the bed. A little farther out of Sebastian's reach. "It's identified that way on purpose. To protect the origin of the salve."

His interests were piqued. He tried to lift himself up onto his elbow, the move manageable, although stiff. "You can trust me."

She laughed. "Can I? I know no such thing. I don't know you at all. All I know is the behemoths took you prisoner. Clearly they beat you." Her hand waved over Sebastian and his makeshift hospital bed. "And something horrible happened to everyone in the room with you. Care to tell me about that?"

"Not particularly, no. Not my first choice."

"Then you can be content with not knowing more about the salves used to treat you." She smiled, tilted her head, and turned with a bob.

Sebastian grimaced, a poor attempt at a frown. He didn't feel the two situations stood on the same ground.

She took one step, paused, and looked back at Sebastian, an uncertain look on her face. The air in the room swirled, a mini cyclone appearing in the space before her. Her muscles tensed. Sebastian pushed himself to a sitting position. Every muscle, joint, tendon, bone, things he didn't even know existed, howled. Holy Grim's Death.

The swirl of air pulled in dust and dirt from every surface in the room. Darkening and calculating, a shape took form deep within the churning chaos. Alice's chest heaved, her breaths uneven and labored. The Grim Reaper, Death himself, stepped from the whirling mass, and Alice squawked, then slumped backwards.

Sebastian caught her and moved her gently to the bed. Dead weight. Her life force was gone. Sebastian glared at his father. "What did you do that for?"

Sebastian's father stood perfectly straight and proper. Suit, tie, and hat as usual. Shoes a scuff-free gloss black. "She held you captive. I'm here to liberate you. I show no mercy to your captors."

Sebastian held Alice's hand and stared into her eyes. "You got it all wrong. She was kind. She was healing me." He turned her hand back and forth in his own, then reached up and moved her head. "Where is she? Why isn't her soul coming to me?" His hand wrapped around the silver locket she wore, felt the warmth of her life force still trapped within.

"I already sent her away."

Sebastian bolted upright. The locket snapped from her neck and remained clasped in his grip. The room swayed and his hand shot out to steady himself. It found the wall, slick with heavy gray paint, cold to the touch. Don't let him see your pain, Sebastian reminded himself. "Where were you when I actually did need you? I was beaten and held captive by ugly chaos monsters—behemoths." His gaze shifted from his father to Alice's body laid out on the dirty mattress. "Alice's people saved me."

His father looked around the stark room with an air of arrogance. "I didn't know. I only just received word."

Sebastian's eyes narrowed on his father. "Only just? Did Mr. Johnson take a slow stroll on his way to find you? Why didn't he do something rather than jot little notes and leave?"

"Johnson does things by the book. I told him to watch; he watched. Now come, let's go. I must get you somewhere safe." He swung his arm out, motioning Sebastian to come along.

Sebastian didn't move. He stared at his father, a storm of heated emotions clashing within him. Fury, frustration, hopelessness, sorrow, and shock, to name a few. "But Johnson, he—"

Sebastian's father jerked his head. It was a signal he wanted to go, not talk. "Yes, yes. Stopped you from foolishness with the dragon. That was the directive. Like I said, he's a by-the-book Reaper. Good man." Sebastian scoffed. "Now come along."

Sebastian still made no motion to leave. "What of Alice?" Sebastian adjusted the woman's arms, making them rest comfortably upon her quiet body. Carefully, he knelt and retrieved the bottle of ointment. Her locket still dangled in his palm. Unsure why he did it, Sebastian shoved the locket in his pocket. Maybe it was guilt. Maybe he would search out her family later, as he had yet to finish for Sophie.

"She is gone. There is nothing more to do." Mortifier grabbed Sebastian and pulled him away from Alice.

"You want me safe?" Sebastian laughed. "What do you care?"

"I care plenty. Someone or something is killing supernaturals. I don't want you to be next."

Sebastian froze, all of his muscles tightening. He pulled back on his father's grip. "What do you mean? Who has died?"

The Grim's eyes fluttered to a lazy close. "Does it matter?"

"It does to me!"

"So far, nothing more than a few dragons. But dragons are not easily conquered. The killer likely has the taste for it now. I've seen it happen many times through the years. More often with the humans, but it happens within the lines of a supernatural species, as well. He will move on, looking for more challenges. Some that will provide cunning and strong opponents. Do you see now? See why I must get you out of this place?" He took hold of Sebastian's arm and pulled him toward the vortex.

Sebastian struggled, but every bit of fight sent him another burning notch up the agony scale. "I really don't see it, Dad." Sebastian spit the title out with venom. "I just killed an entire room full of demons, and I didn't even mean to. Why would anyone, or thing, want to take on a Reaper?"

His father's eyes lit up. "You did? Congratulations, my boy." His hand came down in a solid pat on the back. Sebastian bolted his mouth shut, locking his jaw.

"Alice." The call rang out from the other room, the sound of footsteps approaching.

Sebastian's head snapped to the right and watched a dark-skinned man walk around the corner into the room. The official tag on his breast pocket read B. Crane. He hesitated at the sight of Sebastian and his father.

"Necessary?" Mortifier asked.

Sebastian clutched the bottle of medicine to his chest and returned the stare of the man in the doorway. "What?"

"As I thought," said the Reaper and flicked his finger. The man stumbled back into the hallway and crumbled to the floor. Sebastian didn't have to ask. The guy was dead.

"What is wrong with you?" Sebastian groaned. He wanted to yell, but lacked the necessary strength.

"You say that like it's a bad thing. This is a Reaper's way. Embrace it, Sebastian."

"A Reaper's way," Sebastian mocked. "Not this Reaper's way!" Sebastian hunched his shoulders. "At least, not the way I want to be," he mumbled.

"Stop us, then," his father said, and pulled Sebastian by the arm into the vortex. With a swish, he removed them from the rebel's hideout. As Sebastian observed the white and gray swirls of dust and air spin around him, he watched the dank room where he'd been start to fade. More rebels rushed into the room, gathered around their fallen comrade.

One soldier looked up and pointed to Sebastian and Mortifier as they began to fade in the dissipating swirl of Grim transportation. That was it. That was the moment. All heads turned toward them, a couple pointing. He was now a suspect. It was clear they thought he killed the guy in the doorway. Probably Alice, too. Intimidating men rushed at the vortex. It was a moment of truth. Sebastian could stay and face the consequences, or leave with his father. He remained steadfast, and everything swirled into a churning mess of last-stop destination. Imminent collision with Alice's co-conspirators quickly passing.

Sebastian's gut twisted, a strongman's weight plummeting into his stomach. He threw off his father's hold and crashed straight through the churning chaos and whirling mist wall, directly out of the conveyor-cyclone into the darkening mass beyond.

7

UNFORESEEN

Alice had packed something white and gooey against Sebastian's wound, used a gauze bandage for binding. The salve wasn't working fast enough for his convenience. He wished for a quick heal or quick death. Either should erase the exploding pain in his side. At this point, he wasn't sure he cared which came for him.

Lights blurred in and out, and the rancid smell of piss and beer assaulted him. What time is it? he wondered. Maybe early dawn or the break of night? He leaned forward, reached out, hoping to find a firm hold, something to steady himself. He wasn't disappointed. Cold brick met his palm. He was standing at the corner of an alleyway.

The path from where he stood to where he wanted to go felt daunting, almost undoable. He wasn't sure why he'd come here. Maybe it was his need to tie up loose ends. Damn his nobility. He thought he had been concentrating on Alice. Sophie must have been lingering in his subconscious. When he'd broken free from his dad, jumped into the abyss, he could have gone anywhere. Should have gone to Kyra, but he hadn't.

He was standing beside the now-familiar apartment building filled with broken souls, and stuffed somewhere within were Sophie's parents. The building's side entrance blew open. Four people stammered out, two guys and two girls. One of the guys tossed a bottle to the side, the sound of breaking glass following. He laughed and wrapped his arm around the nearest girl, leaving the shattered bottle at the base of the door.

"Classy tenants," Sebastian mumbled, then frowned, memories of the green Impala and the alleyway beating racing across his mind.

Before the door closed and clasped shut, Sebastian staggered forward and caught the edge, stopping it with fingers sandwiched between door and jamb. Heavy as it was—metal, thick, and wide—it swung easily on its hinges, allowing Sebastian into the space of the building beyond.

He didn't harbor any expectation of what lay inside the door. If he had bothered to visualize the interior, what he found was a pretty good fit. Pattern-heavy carpet, old and worn, running up the wall three or four inches. Dingy and scraped beige walls, and several feet in from the entrance, down a not-too-wide hallway, one small elevator.

Sebastian rested his weight against the wall near the elevator and waited. Waited to push the button. Waited for his head to clear. Waited for an ounce of strength to return. Needing his faculties working well enough for him to get the job done.

Sadness, anger, desire, frustration—a whole flurry of emotion washed over him, and none of it was his. Each one came hand-in-hand with thoughts and memories from the tenants in the building. He was drowning in feelings, and he didn't understand if this severity of the curse was Reaper or Mara in nature. How could either species deal with this constant onslaught? His mind had been so quiet. Why had it all come back with such brutality?

He doubled over and vomited on the carpet.

"Oh man. The night's too young for you to be that wasted." A teenage boy bent down and looked Sebastian in the eye, his hair dropping across his face, obscuring one of his eyes. "What time you start the party?"

Sebastian shifted to better see him, noticed the dark bottle he held.

"Here, let me help you." The boy placed his hand on Sebastian's arm.

"I'm fine," Sebastian said under his breath, and turned to fully meet his would-be helper. Wiping his mouth with the back of his hand, he stared past the teen to the doors of the elevator beyond. The machine groaned as it lumbered up several stories. The sound separated into an army of colorful bangs, clangs, and shrilling echoes. Sebastian wanted to throw his hands over his ears and scream at the world to stop, just stop!

The boy tugged on Sebastian's arm.

"I said I was fine!" Sebastian snapped and swung his arm, pushing the boy away.

The boy banged into the wall on the opposite side of the hall. His bottle dropped, its contents spilling onto the carpet. He glowered at Sebastian before taking off down the hall at a run. He crashed through the entrance, letting the door swing to a close with a hard bang.

Sebastian dropped to the floor and pulled his knees into his chest. He stared at the bottle left behind and thought of Talia's mind helper—Spiritual Peace. Before he realized what he was doing, he was reaching across the hall, grabbing the bottle, and sucking down the last few drops.

He closed his eyes and waited. Only liquor, not a magical elixir. A sigh the weight of his soul swept through him, and he pulled all the anger and frustration he felt inward, until it was the size of a pin prick. He had never been so out of control of his emotions. Not since before he'd run away to the carnival. Before he'd left his father.

He laughed, but there was no heart in the action. It was irony. He had let his father back into his life, and with him came the same landslide of shit. Sitting there for a breath or two, as he did, Sebastian wondered how he could kill a Grim.

Heat settled around him, wavered in the air beside him like a gentle companion, and Sebastian realized he now heard nothing. The usual creak of a door or the squawk of a voice carrying down the hall still held fast, but the feelings and memories lingered no longer. "How?" he said to the vacant hall, tilting the empty bottle in his hand and giving it a scrutinizing glare. Surely it wasn't—

Then his back straightened and eyes widened. Anger. Anger was his key. Possibly even anger at his father, specifically. He wasn't sure, not yet. But he would find out.

The elevator door opened with a long scratch and an old lady stepped out, small dog yanked by a leash at her back. She wrinkled her nose at Sebastian, hugged the far side of the hallway, and walked by quickly. The doors to the elevator started to rattle shut.

No. Sebastian pulled himself up and pushed away from the wall. *I need to be on that.* He threw his ragged body into the cold, tight space moments before the doors closed. Folding himself into the front corner, Sebastian crouched and listened to the silence. There was nothing—no rattle, no hum, no movement of any kind—but a pulse, slow and steady, up on the third floor. He reached over and hit the button for number three. The elevator jolted and began its ascent.

Thump, cha-boom. The elevator halted in a bang, the doors opening with a slow pause-and-go. Sebastian was on the third floor, what he sought—Sophie's family line—to the right. A sluggish beacon summoned him. Shoulder dragging along the wall, left foot schlepping in a tow-and-drop, he moved like a dead man walking. The wall as his crutch.

Outside the apartment, he paused, caught his breath, and took stock of himself. His torn and blood-covered shirt. His dirty, skinned knuckles. With hands shaking and moving deliberately slow, Sebastian zipped the front of his jacket closed, then pulled the sleeves down to hide as much of his hands as possible.

He fought callously to keep his gift stifled, but holding on to anger was harder to do than he had imagined. The emotions and memories kept trying to slither back in to his psyche. Never before had he felt so overwhelmed, so tangled in the struggle for control. Maybe this was his father's intention all along. By keeping Sebastian from the carnival and the aid Talia provided long enough, he was forced to deal.

Sebastian fumed, the heat rising up his neck into his face. Mortifier didn't know what it was like. He couldn't. The Grim was all Reaper. He didn't have to deal with the Mara's gift—or curse, as Sebastian saw it. Sebastian wondered how the two supernatural gifts really affected him. He suspected he got something close to a double dose of overwhelming emotions and memories. Either that, or the Reapers were highly effective in handling the onslaught. Sebastian had a long, cracked road ahead of him before he would learn to master the assault. It seemed impossible. Anger for his father boiled over. All the pain and heartache flashed before his eyes in big, ugly blotches.

And then there was silence. He'd managed it again. Pure resentment of his father had sucked in all the unwanted emotions and memories. The hallway was quiet. Sebastian took a deep breath and stepped up to the door.

He knocked. Waited.

No answer came. But he heard sounds on the other side of the door.

It sounded—Sebastian leaned into the doorframe—it sounded like a mad scurry. A rush of some sort. The noise moved toward him, and Sebastian stepped back, keeping a hand on the frame for balance. The door swung open, exposing a middle-aged woman with blonde, frizzy hair, pulled back tight, accentuating the lines at the corners of her eyes.

"Oh," she said, and set down a recklessly folded box on the table beside the door. "I was expecting someone else. Can I help you?" She brushed at her clothing and tiny bits of paper fluttered to the floor. It looked as if she had been shredding documents. A lot of them, to create that kind of paper fluff. "Did Jon send you?" She turned and walked back into the apartment.

Sebastian shifted his weight, made no move to follow the woman into the space of her apartment. He didn't like the way she so carelessly turned her back on a stranger. Maybe if Sophie had witnessed better behaviors at home, from her family, she might not have ended up dead with Lance-the-loser.

"You're not a vampire, are you?" she called back to him. "Waiting for some kind of invite to come in?"

"I don't feel right." Sebastian leaned against the door. Is she serious? Sebastian found himself dialing back his anger, wanting to let his ability free so he could feel her emotions, understand what she did and didn't know.

"It's fine, honey. If Jon sent you, there's no worry." She fussed a few feet away with boxes, stuffing things in, closing them up.

"Jon didn't send me."

She stopped and turned to look at him. "Oh, my. How rude of me. I just assumed—"

Sebastian took one step through the door. "I'm here about your daughter. I do have the right place, don't I?" He glanced around the apartment. Items that gave a home a personal touch were conveniently absent. "You do have a daughter, right?"

"Oh, my," she said again. "Yes, I'm sorry." She stood, took two steps toward him. "Of course, it was she who sent you—"

Sebastian braved another step, closing the gap even more. "Sophie wanted, or rather, she requested—"

"Sophie?" A puzzled look replaced the focus the woman had worn as a formfitting mask. Her body froze and shoulders slumped. "What of—?"

Sebastian's hand dropped over the curve of her left shoulder before she could say another word. "She has an important message for you." Before the last of his words even touched the air, a stream of impressions, feelings, and desires leaped from his fingertips and rushed through the woman's bloodstream, straight to her head, heart, and soul. Sophie's message of peace, love, and forgiveness swept through her mother's entire being like an unexpected flood. No corner of her conscience was left untouched. Her knees gave way to the weight of revelation and she collapsed, Sebastian catching her in his arms. The flood continued, only now it was a cyclone of emotion coming from Sophie's mom—anguish and anger, understanding. She sighed and cried into his arms, accepting a truth she could not change. But there was something else—

Sebastian held her and attempted to comfort her. All the while, his eyes searched for that something, the something he'd picked out of her memories. The very something kicking his adrenaline into a top-speed spin.

He knew the moment he'd found it. On the wall, in a basic oak frame, hung a faded picture mounted on what probably used to be red construction paper. A very young Sophie stood beside a man, huge grins on their faces, a Christmas tree in the background. Across the top in kid-scribbled Crayola, it read Santa brought me a daddy for Christmas. Jon B Davies. On the other side of Jon Davies was another girl. A bit older than Sophie, she stood a tad taller and had her blonde hair pulled back in a pony.

Alice.

Sebastian's mind summersaulted. He took a step back, dragging Sophie's mom with him.

She pulled herself together and looked at him, confusion and knowing burning in her eyes. "What of Alice?" she said.

Shit. Sebastian dropped his arms, took another step back. His hand reached into his pants pocket, felt for Alice's locket. Wrapped it securely in his grasp. He should give it to the woman, Alice's mother—he knew that—but for the first time since he'd started his Reaping gig, he was petrified. This woman had lost not one, but two daughters, and the blame for one could partially fall on his own head. He took another step back, another step toward the door.

"Where are you going?" she questioned. "You can't leave. You need to explain yourself. Explain this." She waved her hands between them, implying the memory and emotion exchange that had just taken place.

"I'm sorry. I'm so, so sorry. But I can't." Sebastian turned and scuttled out the door. His body protested, argued his decision to run, but he fought against it, pushed his physical limits and bolted down the hall. She yelled at his back, but he didn't turn to look, and he couldn't hear her over the labored beat of his heart. His hand slammed on the elevator button, flattening against the surrounding cold metal plate, depressing both the up and down options together.

The doors opened almost immediately. In his haste to escape, Sebastian glanced at Sophie and Alice's mom coming down the hall after him and stepped through the opening, taking notice far too late the elevator wasn't sitting in wait.

Sebastian twisted and fell into the dark elevator shaft.

8

CRIMP

By the light of day, Club Afterlife lacked that special something that made it popular with the crowds by nightfall. Marcus stood in the middle of the dance floor and stared past the pool tables to the large entertainment balcony beyond. He thought of the first night he'd brought Kyra here, how everything had gone so much better than he had anticipated. Losing her memory had been unforeseen, but so damn perfect. Now look at the mess Marcus had to deal with. He shook his head. What had Leila been thinking, bringing Sebastian here?

"Well, let's see it," Marcus said, and turned to meet Rick's waiting, watchful eye.

Rick pivoted, did an about-face, and led the way to a private staircase. Bright and stark was the stairwell, its main purpose the flow of supplies. They descended several flights, passing various levels of the club along the way to the basement. Heavy, dark scuffs, trash, and blood littered the last several steps before they walked through the door into the open storage area. The large metal door to the area beyond remained open, and men worked in the dank space with high-powered hoses, spraying the walls and floors. Where Marcus and Rick stood, several bodies had been tossed in a pile to the side. Someone had scrubbed and cleaned up the rest of the wreckage already.

Rick stopped and his gaze swept over the place, his lips twisting to the side.

"How many were there?" Marcus asked.

"According to the surveillance playback, about a dozen or so," Rick said with a mild nod of the head.

"A dozen," Marcus repeated, his tone dry, surly. "A dozen men, and we only manage to take out three of them, while losing all our own?" His nostrils flared.

Rick took a step back. "Well..." He pointed to the busy cleanup in the next room. "Something we can't explain went down."

"What happened?" Marcus's eyes narrowed, then he stared past Rick and walked through the door to the other room. The large cage stood at the far end. A guy whose name he hadn't bothered to learn was hosing the area down. Chunks of matter—flesh and blood—were pushed into piles by the water spray. "What in all dragons' domain happened here?"

"That's the thing. We're not sure. The surveillance turned to static right after the first shots rang out. There's no way of telling without getting ahold of an actual witness."

"Then get me a fucking witness," Marcus snarled. "I want to know what killed my men." He stood rigid, felt the fury burning through his bloodstream. If the Mara bastard was responsible—

Marcus spun around and stormed back to the front room, to the pile of bodies waiting there. He kicked at the one on top, watched it topple over. Dark fatigues. No distinguishing markings on the clothing—but for one tiny little square of an emblem, a patch sewn to the lower left corner of the soldier's vest. Easily overlooked. Marcus growled.

"So. He found me." Marcus raked his hand through his hair and kicked the soldier again, for extra measure.

"It would seem so, sir," Rick said, stepping up beside him. "But they didn't seem as interested in where you were, as in what was behind this door." He pointed to the large metal brute hanging wide open. "May I ask what, or who, you had locked up?"

Marcus turned sharply, stared right down at Rick. "No, you may not." He pivoted and walked for the stairwell. "I want all this cleaned up before the club opens, and I want Davies and his silly army found and destroyed. Understood?"

"Of course. But shouldn't Chet be here? Isn't this his territory?"

"I have Chet working on another matter. Never mind about him." Marcus paused in the doorway, looked back over the mess. "And get me Leila on the phone. I want to have a chat with her."

"Sir?"

"Just do it." Marcus stomped up the stairs, his feet coming down on each step with a heavy clang. His mind was calculating, deciphering, planning. If Davies was on to him, then it was time to use Davies to his advantage. This was nothing more than a crimp in his otherwise perfect plan. The edges of Marcus's lips twitched and lifted, warm contempt spreading through his chest like a plague.

9
DOWNTIME

The black of the elevator shaft moved past Sebastian's falling body at incredible speed. Soon he'd be broken bits on the bottom floor.

And then he wasn't. The swirl of a Reaper's vortex rose around him, encircled him, pulled him in. Next thing he knew, he was laying on a foggy forest floor.

How had he done that? Sebastian wasn't sure, but he wanted to know. There were so many things he wanted to know. He stared at the branches of the trees above him for a breath or five before forcing himself to move. Everything within him protested when he pushed up on his elbows, stood, and took a step. He recognized where he was, though, and the prospects of a more comfortable resting place propelled him.

Red and blue and purple, a rainbow of colored lines aglow. They flashed and swirled, running in loops, dips, and high mountain climbs. Sebastian used them as a guide through the fog, stumbling on the first step into the clear. The puncture in his side screamed mercy. It slowed his pace beyond his liking. He thought of Kyra and an ache churned in his chest. He should be seeking her out, making sure she was safe, but he wouldn't be much help to her in his present condition. If anything, he'd probably bring her more trouble. And so he'd found himself shuffling through the fog. The damn, irritating fog.

Still—Kyra was a dragon, and according to his father, dragons were dying!

He pinned his gaze upon the small funnel cake cart near the front of the carnival's entrance. Madame Rue didn't see him. Soon enough, she would. He would make sure she couldn't avoid him. He planned to hit the side of the thing and collapse. Then she would see him and get help. Somebody was bound to make sure Sebastian got to his tarot card trailer and his bed. All he needed was a few hours of sleep. He'd awake in better shape. He felt sure of it.

Sebastian.

His name whispered through the lingering crowd. Unsure if he'd actually heard it or not, Sebastian looked to his left, and then to his right. Zeke sat in his usual spot on the bench by the quiet river. Or was it a lake? So hidden by the mist, no one was sure how far the water extended.

Entertaining the idea of joining the old blind man lasted a mere millisecond. Sebastian seriously wanted for his bed. Zeke waved, and Sebastian found himself waving back. He paused, his face wrinkling. It made no sense to wave at a blind man. His hand came down on the edge of the funnel cake cart. The delicious aroma of batter and strawberries mixed with a metallic smell. It was wrong, and it turned his stomach. He knew it meant a shift in the carnival. Things were about to move, like they often did. It was part of the allure of Mystic's Carnival—the magic. Things were always shifting and moving, pathways changing. One could never be certain of their direction. The carnival knew where people needed to go, and it led them there. Where you wound up wasn't always where you wanted to go, but you got where you needed to be.

Tiny sparks began to fizzle and pop in the atmosphere, and the support beneath Sebastian's hands vanished. He faltered, taking a step to catch himself. His shin connected with something hard, mid-bone.

"Gotcha."

A hand grabbed him. The pain sliced through him, the support pressing too close to his wound.

"Have a seat," Zeke said.

Sebastian plopped down on the bench beside the old codger. "Nothing personal, but I'd much rather be in bed right now than hanging with you."

Zeke folded his hands over his cane and looked out toward the funnel cake cart and the entrance portal beyond. Sebastian knew the old man wasn't seeing any of it, but it didn't matter. "Tired, are you?"

Sebastian slumped in his spot, unsure how long he'd be able to hold a conversation, or himself, up. "Very."

"Haven't seen much of you since Higgins's service. What have you been up to?"

Sebastian's thoughts ran through the memories of Higgins. His sacrifice for Kyra, his service, what Zeke had asked of Sebastian after Higgins's death, what Sebastian had ultimately done for them both. Sebastian had learned so much about the Higgins and the phoenix that cold, rainy day. He looked toward the busy carnival and wondered what it was he had seen when he'd pulled Higgins's body out of purgatory. What it had meant for the old man. "The usual. Keeping myself busy, that's all."

Sebastian rested his elbow on the arm of the bench and let himself fall against it, supporting himself by one hand pressed against his cheek.

Zeke cleared his throat. "See Madame Rue, there?" Sebastian turned his gaze back to the funnel cake cart. "She also misses Higgins, and Kyra. She throws herself into her work as a means of coping. Is that what you are doing?"

Sebastian took a deep breath. He wanted to close his eyes and not open them again for an eternity of time. He fought the desire, and instead looked back at Zeke. "Do you think I'm avoiding dealing with things? Because if so, you're way off base. I'm going to get Kyra back. She is in need of help and I'm going to bring her that help. I merely need to recoup first."

Zeke's head bobbed up and down slowly. "Good. Good. I have faith you will do right by her."

"I'm glad somebody does."

Zeke's hand squeezed Sebastian's, stirring him from a complacent state. "You must believe in yourself and trust your gut."

Sebastian stared at Zeke's hand. How does he always know

exactly where to reach? "I'm just feeling a little defeated at the moment, and all I want to do right now is hole up and lick my black hole of a wound."

Zeke's head turned in Sebastian's direction. "And how is that going to help Kyra?"

Sebastian's defenses raised a degree. "How can I help her when I'm mangled and torn to shreds? I can hardly walk without doubling over."

Zeke patted Sebastian's hand, his face and eyes loosening in an open and warm manner. "Alright, my boy. Alright," he said, his voice gentle.

Sebastian felt his insides turn to cinder. He despised himself, his damn inability to protect and save Kyra. He should have broken the rules that day in purgatory, seen her safely back to the living. He was already breaking the rules by being there and helping her. She never should have landed in the hospital with no memory of who or what she was. And she certainly shouldn't be in a relationship with any man morally capable of what Marcus had done to Sebastian. Marcus was a complete dickhead.

If only he understood Marcus's motives.

"The answer is often right in front of you. You only need know where to look."

Zeke's words were spoken so quietly it was a wonder Sebastian heard them. Though he suspected Zeke knew he'd hear, regardless of the low volume. Despite his exhaustion, Sebastian's mind started running over everything he knew regarding Kyra's situation. There had to be something. Something he was missing.

"What are you fellas up to?"

Chelsea was walking their way. She wore a delicate smile and the usual white dressing gown, featuring a flared base along the bottom four or so inches of the skirt, puffy sleeves, and vintage medallion lace. Today she also wore a light blue robe with a princess waist tie and slippers to match. She usually showed up in her night attire, like she'd crawled out her window after retiring to her room. Or out the hospital room window. Wherever it was she was staying these days. If only Sebastian had known the young cancer girl would become a permanent fixture in his life, he might have handled things differently the day he had given her a reprieve from death.

He hated getting to know her. Hated that she tried to make him care. It would make things more difficult, more painful later, when he was called to reap her soul. There would be no third chance for her. The cancer slowly chomped away at her anatomy. Her Grim bell would soon chime.

"We were only talking, child." Zeke reached back and patted Sebastian on the back. "I'm sure this young man would enjoy your company immensely."

Sebastian shot Zeke a what-the-hell look. Even if the old man wasn't aware of how Sebastian felt, the prompt was uncool. He wanted to crash, and that Zeke did know.

"Chelsea, hon." Zeke's hand reached in her direction and shook in the air. "Why don't you see Sebastian to his trailer?"

Zeke's dark skin vibrated in front of Sebastian; it was all he focused on. Everything else blurred at the edges. He didn't hear Chelsea's response. Her words blended with the hum and roar of the carnival crowd beyond the gates. He felt the desire to yak churning in his stomach.

Planting his hand firmly on the bench arm, Sebastian steadied himself and began to stand. "If you see Talia, can you ask her to swing by my place?" Sebastian didn't know the odds of Zeke running into Talia, but the forever-present carnival visitor sure had a way of knowing everyone and everything in the most magical way. Sebastian needed to talk to the young witch about Kyra, and felt confident Zeke would make it happen.

He stood, his weight shifting, muscles straining, pain pulsing sharply through his core. White dots popped into his vision. They expanded quick and enveloped all the cosmos. Sebastian lurched forward, throwing a foot out to stop and correct his maneuver. It failed. He teetered to the side and succumbed to gravity.

A groan hissed from between his lips, the grass racing toward his face at a tilt.

"Oh!" Chelsea hurried to close the distance. Her hands came

into view seconds later.

His vision dimmed. Then it was gone. All gone.

*****

Dancing midnight, like black silk waving in a breeze atop a silver mesh, floated above. The Mara Web. It was an impenetrable cloud cover, spanning as far as Sebastian could see. There was no escape, only net. Beneath him, soft ground mimicked his bed. It moved, molding itself to his form. His body trembled, unwilling to move, and a trickle of sweat ran down his temple. The only sky visible below the dangerous sky-high trap flowed in dark squiggles of purples and grays.

Sebastian stared at the shimmering crisscross pattern of the Mara snare, reason dictating in his ear, reminding him to be terrified. Of all the things he'd come across, the Mara Web made him the most vulnerable. But tonight his logic switch had flipped to off, because Sebastian felt oddly at ease among the foreign terrain. No tension existed. He only wanted tranquility. Sleep.

As far as his average dream went, this one was seriously strange. But there was so much about Mara nature he had yet to understand. His mother hadn't exactly been the nurturing type, and when she'd left, he was a mere three years of age.

He closed his eyes. Only for a short while, he promised himself. He'd rest for a few minutes—fifteen or so—then he'd explore the new dream world. After his energy returned. He took a deep breath and released the tension he'd been holding. Warmth radiated across his body, generated from the pulsating pain in his abdomen.

What happens to the dreamer if he dreams within an already active dream? The curious notion had barely taken form in Sebastian's synapses when the memory of the mesh above faded into a crowded sky of flapping wings. Dragons. They covered the celestial sphere. Flying in swirling mists of burning embers. He couldn't blink, couldn't look away. It was mesmerizing.

Extraordinary numbers for a supposed dying race.

Something pushed against his leg. Flushed and firm, it pressed, gliding up his body in one long, fluid motion. The something was a someone, and she was devastating and stunning and Mara. Her appeal went beyond exquisite. No doubt, Mara-magically conceived. The first Mara Sebastian had seen since his mother. The mother who hadn't wanted him.

Curvaceous bohemian dream: raven hair, cherry bruised lips, and eyes that even the devil would work to please. Sebastian pushed up on his elbows and his breath caught in his chest.

"Relax," her voice sang, washing over him like soothing bathwater.

He wanted to obey, and that made him feel weak. I'm not merely Mara, he reminded himself. I am Reaper. Somehow that had to make him stronger. Didn't it? He detested himself for succumbing, if only one inch or one millisecond, to her Mara call. His head shook, fighting the effects, fighting to knock her hooks free. But look away, he would not. Miss the chance to witness or study or question a Mara? Wasn't gonna happen.

"Don't fight. Give in to the pleasure. Let us happen." She glided up his body, her hands exploring everything, every inch of the way. She left nothing sacred, nothing to the imagination. "You are the only son of the nightmare, in a faction populated by daughters. I've wanted so terribly long to know you."

A violent cough burst from Sebastian's lungs. The craving for water helped him rein in his focus, fight the power of the Mara. Push her away or scramble out from beneath her was what he'd do if he were in full form. But he wasn't at his best, and there was no telling what would set her off. Sebastian straightened his back, pushing farther up onto his elbows. She shoved him down and pinned him to the ground before he could take a breath. Bullets ricocheted like wild shrapnel, bouncing through his shoulder blades and ribcage. He grimaced.

All that move revealed was Sebastian had a damn inconvenient, drawn-out healing process to complete. Nothing new was gained from his pain. A different method needed to be employed.

Delving deep within his soul, Sebastian explored the darker corners of his mind—the playgrounds reserved for dreams and nightmares. Pulling forth his Mara, he let the spectacular beast seep into everything—every move he made, every breath he took, every word he spoke. "I've been keeping a low profile. How did you find out about me?"

A deliciously crooked smile crept across her face. "Oh honey, something like you can't exist and there not be talk. People hear things. I hear everything." Her hand moved to the most sensual and sensitive of areas, her fingers caressing the curve of his groin. Sebastian froze, every muscle going rigid. "Imagine if I were to sit on you instead of some waste of a human." She straddled him with the speed of sudden, urgent desire. Her body immediately slow danced, so hot, so moist. "What would we create together?" She bent forward, bringing her lips close to his, rolling her breath across his cheek.

He closed his eyes and turned his head away. Fucking hell, the pictures she was bombarding him with. The things she wanted to tempt him with. All the things she imagined them doing. He'd never dreamed the Mara magic was this intense or abusive. Sebastian started to pull away, drag himself out from beneath her weight.

A ripple ran over her figure. It morphed her dark hair to red. "I can look like anyone or anything you desire."

Sebastian was staring into Kyra's eyes. The Mara had taken her face. He wasn't fooled, and yet—part of him wanted to be. He could pretend, if only for the length of a dream, and he would have Kyra.

He shook his head and pushed her away. It wasn't Kyra. She wasn't Kyra, and she never would be. "Get off," he yelled. "You are not her. Don't pretend to be."

The Mara shed her Kyra disguise. The dark-haired beauty once again sat atop him, overpowering him. "You don't like it?"

"No, I don't. You are forbidden to take the form of another girl."

She smirked, her smile taking on a wicked curve. The kind

Sebastian had become all too familiar with after his time spent working the carnival. She placated him with little to no conviction in her stature. "Very well. You can see how we are meant to be, can't you? Mara-à-Mara. It couldn't be more ideal."

Sebastian wasn't so sure. Although—he could learn a lot from spending time with someone of the same nature. That didn't mean he wanted to get personal with her. No way in Reaper's hell.

He scratched the back of his neck and scrunched his brow. "I suspect a Mara is involved in a small matter I'm having trouble with currently. You wouldn't know anything about that, would you?"

She torqued her head to the side, batted her thick lashes, and brushed her lips along his jawline. "What answer will result in us working together?" Before he could blink, she was on him again, pushing him down and pressing pelvis to pelvis in a slow grind.

The blood rush was quick, the hardening unstoppable. Not with her, he thought. Not with her. He shoved her away and yelled, "No! I am stronger than you. I am a Reaper!"

He bolted awake.

*****

Chelsea sat across the room in his favorite comfy chair. Momentarily disoriented, Sebastian didn't say a thing, didn't move, simply searched the small trailer with a sweeping gaze. The dream came to him like a car slamming into a telephone pole. He pushed up onto his elbows. "How long have I been asleep?"

Chelsea bit her lip and delivered a timid smile. "A few hours."

Swinging his legs over the side of the bed, he sat up. His trailer was tiny. There were only a few feet between the top of his head and the ceiling.

Chelsea leaned forward in her seat. "What's wrong?"

Sebastian stretched his shoulders and released. He no longer felt pain from his wound. "A few hours is a few too many." He looked down and lifted his shirt. The bandage was new. He looked around the tiny space and stopped at the blood-soaked gauze wadded up and discarded with a small bundle of trash in his wastebasket.

Chelsea followed his gaze. "I hope you don't mind. We took the liberty of cleaning you up and changing your bandage. It looked in need. The old one was in bad shape."

"Who's 'we'?"

"Talia and myself. She came by earlier, said she'd come back."

Sebastian nodded. That was good news. He needed to talk to Talia about Kyra's pendant. Curious, he pulled back the bandage, then glanced at Chelsea.

"It's alright," she said. "It's not anything I haven't already seen."

He suspected not. He had the strangest feeling where Chelsea was concerned. Tension built in his brow and his eyes narrowed in at her, but he didn't see anything screaming guilty, so he looked down at the wound. Only there was no wound. He was completely healed.

"How…?" Sebastian began, then cut off his own words.

"I think it was a combination of things. That stuff you slathered on did a miraculous job fixing you up quick. Zeke said it was the best medicine you could have found. Although, he didn't look too happy about it." Chelsea's lips drew into a tight line. "Then Talia came in with some wild mojo of her own while you were sleeping." Her face lit up. "You should have seen it. There's nothing like it in this world. It was magic!"

Sebastian shook with laughter. "That's most likely what it was. Magic. Talia is a witch."

The small room grew quiet and Chelsea absorbed her "oh-wow" moment. Sebastian could see it was a process for her. He was surprised that with as many visits as she'd made to the carnival, she hadn't come to the realization already. Sebastian chewed on Chelsea's comment. Why was Zeke bothered by the medicine used? Something didn't feel right. Tension crept into his back and shoulders. "What was it, the medicine used on me? Did Zeke say?"

"I have no idea. He didn't mention. I assumed you would know. Said all you needed was some downtime, and you'd be good as new." Chelsea leaned forward in the chair. "You really don't know what it was?"

"Nope. Alice wouldn't—" Sebastian halted mid-sentence. Memories of what his father had done to Alice flooded his mind. Of Alice and Sophie—sisters, both now deceased. He should go to purgatory and look for Alice. Except, if she went directly to one of the destinations beyond purgatory—Heaven or Hell—he wasn't welcome there. His father had made it sound like she'd been sent straight to one of those places. If that's where Alice had gone, there was nothing left to do. No apology could ever be made.

The atmosphere in the trailer thickened, pressing him from every angle, pushing the oxygen straight from his lungs. Ties with his father must be severed. Sebastian needed to get out from under his control. Except, would that mean embracing his Mara half? He wasn't so sure that was the best thing. Sebastian frowned, considering the consequences of cutting his father out of his life. He couldn't do it. Not right this second, anyway.

Now, he needed to focus on the blonde in the dressing gown sitting across from him. "How long have you been sitting here watching me?"

"The whole time, of course." Her answer implied it had been a silly question, with which Sebastian did not agree.

"Why would you sit here that long?"

"Isn't it obvious?" When Sebastian didn't answer, Chelsea continued. "You looked like you were going to die. You had a hole punched through you. A hole! Somebody had to keep an eye on you. Make sure you were healing and not getting worse."

Sebastian shrugged. Her explanation actually made a lot of sense. So did his thought of keeping her outside of his friends circle. Friends. His heart panged at the thought. He yearned for Kyra's return.

Still, it was clear he and Chelsea were fated in at least one way, if not several. He watched her move about the trailer with caution. Black death curled up cozy inside her. It would eventually call them together in an official capacity, and that's exactly why he hated that she'd wiggled her way into his life. He didn't want to feel something meaningful and painful when that day came. But there was something more to the girl. The puzzle of Chelsea had been bothering Sebastian for some time now. Yes, she was dying, but the more needed to be discovered. He didn't like not knowing. It left the door open for unwanted surprises. Only, dealing with her now would slow down his rescue of Kyra, and nothing was more important than Kyra. Not in his world.

Sebastian stood and stepped over to his tiny chest of drawers. "Chelsea, do you live at home?" He grabbed a clean shirt and switched out the tattered, bloodstained one he was wearing. Before closing the drawer, he grabbed a tiny bottle of Talia's Spiritual Peace tonic and shoved it in his pocket with Alice's locket. As a Grim reaps, no doubt he'd be needing a sip or two soon. He glanced at Chelsea. *Funny how I never pick anything up from her.*

"Where else would I live?" Chelsea asked. She sounded perplexed. Sebastian decided she was probably unaware of the severity of her condition. If she knew, she'd probably be in some kind of hospital where she could be treated, as he had envisioned her. It was most likely her unusual cancer that made her a void in a sea of memories and emotions of the dead and dying.

"Maybe you should…" He stopped and looked at her, letting his gaze take in all of her in silence. She deserved better than having her final days void of hope, trapped in an institute, hooked up to machines, slave to a regulated medicine routine. Sometimes ignorance was a blessing. He'd allow her that.

She stared at him expectantly.

He averted his eyes and instead grabbed his jacket off the edge of the bed. "Help me find Talia and my way back to Zeke."

"Looks like you're doing fine on your own." She rose from the chair and took a slow look around. He was doing fine, but he needed an excuse to pull her out of his trailer. Leaving her alone with all his personal belongings was not something he wanted to do. "I finally get to see the inside of your place, and it's so short-lived." She sighed.

He walked toward her. "Sorry." He paused for a moment. "Come on, let's go. I need to talk to Zeke." Sebastian opened the door and stepped into the brisk night, Chelsea instantly at his side providing support.

*****

"Back from the dead, my boy?" Zeke waved Sebastian to the bench. "You had us all concerned. Glad to hear you up and about." Zeke spoke with a mere dash of emotion, and stared at the front gate. He sat on the usual bench, leaning forward on his cane.

Talia jumped in front of Sebastian, bursting from a cloud of smoke. Finger repeatedly jammed in his chest, she poked him and then spun around. "Everyone's all like, dead, Sebastian's dead. I'm all, gah. No way. Watch this." She spun her hands around each other real fast. "Magic delivered." She bowed. Her brown hair sprung from her head in a wild mess, but she was always impeccably clean. Just fashionable Talia with a wild personality, wild hairstyles, and a wild wardrobe.

"Thanks for fixing me, Talia. I'm forever in your debt." Sebastian bowed his head. Working with her was always refreshing. Never the same thing twice.

Talia skipped backwards, toward Zeke on the bench. "You owe me for so many things, pretty boy, I'll be collecting until you collect me."

Right. Sebastian didn't care to think about collecting the souls of the people he knew. Why did Talia have to bring that up? "I need to talk to you."

"Yeah, yeah. Bring it on, hot stuff." She spun in a circle before plopping on an arm of the bench.

"The tooth pendant. The one you told me to look for. Kyra wasn't wearing it."

Talia flicked her fingers together so fast she could probably start fire with the proper friction. "You didn't look hard enough. She has it on her person somewhere. If she ain't wearing it around her neck, then it's someplace else." Talia's face began to twitch. Her eyebrow danced and a wicked little grin snuck across her lips.

"Strip her naked if you need to. You find it."

Sebastian laughed, felt his cheeks warm.

Chelsea coughed.

"Wait," Talia said, and produced a ball of white smoke between her open palms. She studied it for several seconds before waving it away and facing Sebastian. "I had it wrong. Check even closer. It may be deeper than on her person."

"What does that mean?" Sebastian stared at her, confusion and disbelief flooding his system.

Talia slapped him on the back. "Think about it, pretty boy. I'm sure you'll figure it out. You're a smart guy." She danced a couple of steps back, a wicked grin gracing her delicate features.

"You done here? Sebastian and I need to talk." Zeke's tone was neither agitated nor annoyed, but Sebastian felt a psychic push telling him to hurry up.

Sebastian turned toward Chelsea. "Thanks for your help. I really appreciate it, but I've got it from here."

Chelsea looked stunned and disappointed, but didn't argue. "I'm so glad you're going to be fine. I was worried." She kissed him on the cheek and ran from the scene.

Sebastian watched her go. She was a curious girl. Falling for her Reaper. Did her subconscious mind remember he'd let her live when she was supposed to die? Whatever bothered him about her, had he actually created it? His thumb and finger rubbed at his chin, attempting to coax the answer out. Only it wasn't there to be found. He moved toward the bench.

Talia hopped off the bench, pranced around the fringe, and eyed Sebastian. He stood with fists jammed in his pockets and feet planted shoulder width apart, prepared to go to war for the answers he sought. She leaned in with a small piece of folded paper between her fingers, shoved it at his chest. "Here's the deal. Old man there is going to gnaw your ear off, talk to you about... stuff. Listen to him, but add this to your to-do list. Don't forget the dagger." Sebastian's brow pinched, and Talia pointed to the paper. "It's all there. Read it."

"Time's short," Zeke reminded.

Talia jumped on one foot. "I know! This is important." Talia grabbed Sebastian's arm, yanking it free of the pocket. "You're going to thank me for this, too." She winked and began to rub and roll her hands over the bare skin of his forearm.

The friction warmed, sizzled, then roasted his skin. Concentrated in a circle and splaying out along his artery, he melted. He tried to hold still, but damn, it wasn't easy. "Ouch."

"Sorry." She blew lightly across the burn. Something looking spookily like a tattoo now marked up his arm. "This will help you get wherever you need to be." She pointed to the design. "It will lead you to the nearest Gatekeeper, or whatever else you need."

"Gatekeeper?" Sebastian stared at the new art decorating his skin. White lines swung around, creating an elaborate compass of sorts, minus any polar markings.

"For when you need a shortcut."

Sebastian didn't look up, but continued to study the design. Watched the hand within the compass rotate. "I'm familiar with Gatekeepers." When Sebastian finally looked up, Talia was gone.

It was only the two of them now, Sebastian and Zeke. He turned to the old man sitting on the bench and leaning into his cane. May he be as wise as he appeared. Sebastian had questions. Something about dragons, and Kyra was at the cold heart of it. "Let's talk about Kyra."

Zeke smiled.

FORMALITY

W"**here have you been?**" The muscles in Marcus's neck strained. One at the corner of his eye twitched. "You kept me waiting. Never keep me waiting." He paced the Great Hall, his footsteps echoing off the stone interior.

Leila laughed. "Do you think I fear you? It would be foolish to think so. I am the one with the plan. I make the rules." She swept into the room through the main double doors and strolled casually down the cascading staircase. "You must learn patience. Did you never learn its virtues?"

The former decadence of the Great Hall's décor lay in ruin, victim to decades of neglect and abandonment. Once the hottest spot in town, it was now buried beneath the cityscape, forgotten. Only the old and few remembered it, knew of its existence. Knew how to find it.

Five jars sat on the grand staircase. Within each swirled magical storms, each of a different color and origin. The dragons, determined creatures that they were, thrashed at their glass cages with their magical essence and wild determination. They would never give up, never back down. That was one reason Marcus had chosen these particular dragons. Of course, many dragons fit that description. Not all, but many. Finding the right five had been nothing more than a formality. He'd never doubted he would get what he needed, that the convergence would provide for his own dragon's return. And more.

Leila sauntered across the wide, open floor toward him.

"What of your young dragon?"

Marcus's back and shoulders stiffened. He didn't like it when Leila questioned his relationships, but he wouldn't let her know she got under his skin. He stood a smidge taller. "Chet is keeping Kyra entertained tonight. A work night at home. Or some such thing."

"You trust Chet?" A nasty hint of heartless ruination played in her words.

Marcus stood his ground, a stern burn in his stare. "My men would never defy me."

Leila laughed and closed the space between them. "You've been waiting all this time, and you don't have everything prepared? I would have thought you'd have the place prepped and ready to go."

Leila's walk reminded Marcus of a gait. She was too proud. He could fix that.

"Come." She grabbed a torch with one hand, and two candles between her fingers with the other. "Let's get it set up."

Following her lead, they had the symbol created out of candles in a matter of minutes. Marcus walked the circle, lighting each wick in turn. Shadows reached away from the circle laid at their feet. The shadows danced, fading as they blew farther away.

"Put the dragons in the center, aligning them in an arc in front of you," she said, pointing out where she wanted Marcus to place the beasts.

He strode across the room. A smile warmed Marcus's heart as he continued to work, preparing for the ceremony. Setup was going to take some time, but in the end he'd get what no other dragon before him ever had—the power of all species in one. He would be unstoppable.

*****

Simple. Zeke had called retrieving the dagger from the dragon's den an easy task. Easy, my ass, thought Sebastian, and he continued to run at a frantic pace along the country road. It was quiet, almost too still. No one around for as far as the eye could see. He couldn't believe he hadn't found a portal yet.

Actually, that was a lie.

The little white lines of the compass etched into his forearm burned, the arrow within continuously spinning around and around, never pausing long enough to indicate a direction in which he should tread. Just his luck—the new gate gizmo wasn't working. He'd been so sure there would be a Gatekeeper down this stretch of road. If only he could find a member. Any tired old member would do.

No. Scratch that.

The Gatekeeper needed to be young and inexperienced. The less experience, the more likely to bend, even break the rules, and that's what he was looking for tonight.

Sebastian shivered, recalled Zeke's words. Zeke wanted Sebastian to find Bolsvck. One of the most powerful dragons still alive. Yeah, that wasn't dangerous. Grim chance he would make time for a Reaper. Yet Bolsvck was the only one worthy of challenging Marcus, according to Zeke, so somehow Sebastian had to get to him. Had to enlist his help. And he was Kyra's father, so that had to count for something.

How much does Zeke really know? Sebastian wondered.

Sebastian had no time to waste, yet he was losing time looking for someone who didn't want to be found. Gatekeepers died, didn't they? He should be able to feel their souls, yet all he got was some kind of fuzzy resonance. It pinpointed a rather large area and gave him nothing more. Far too general. He had no clue what the distorted feeling meant, and Talia's gift—the compass—wasn't helping at all. To be privy to his father's vast knowledge would be a godsend, if only Sebastian knew a way to absorb it all in one sitting.

He laughed out loud. So much knowledge at once would likely overwhelm him. Possibly turn his brain to pulverized roadkill. As this venture was likely to do. Dragons weren't known for their common courtesy, and there was a reason Kyra had run away to the carnival. Sebastian hoped Zeke knew what he was doing, sending Sebastian in search of Kyra's father. Something told him she wasn't going to like this when she got her memories back.

Sebastian stopped, braced his hands on his knees, and took a long breath. Running along the road wasn't working. There had to be something else. Something better. He had to think like a Gatekeeper. Look for them where they would most likely be. Of all the gates Sebastian knew of, none were on a main thoroughfare. Not ever. Gates were always hidden away, off to the side, in quiet places less likely to be traveled and observed.

Hordes of bats flooded his insides. The pressure of time was his enemy, stressing his mind, messing with his thought process and making each minute feel more dire.

He closed his eyes, cleared his mind, and said a silent prayer. More like a wish, but he hoped someone was listening enough to care. Unclear to him was whether the higher powers bothered with prayers from Reapers. Didn't stop him from trying.

If his gut was telling him which way to go, he wished it would scream. Subtle whispers weren't working for him. A gentle whisper seemed to be all he was getting, though. He couldn't even be sure it meant anything, but he followed. Turning to the left, he ran from the road, deep into the woods.

Each stride sank with a heavy foot upon the dirt path, and the farther along he moved, the more confident he felt. "Come on, Gatekeeper," he mumbled. "Show me where you are." The words had no sooner left his lips than the compass locked in on a location and pointed the way.

Ghastly Grim! Could it have been so simple all along? Why didn't he think to ask for the location out loud? He cursed himself, shook his head, and moved forward through the brush.

A natural path came in from the left and curved, merging with his direction of motion. He followed the pathway and it remained steady with the compass reading. Wide enough for one at first, it narrowed to something small animals had likely made. Barely noticeable unless you were looking hard to see the route.

He pushed his way through, moving branches and sweeping around bushes. It was the longest, most drawn-out moment of his life. That he could recall, anyway. He'd probably been running for twenty minutes, but it felt like sixty. A small watering hole lay at the end of the path. An ideal location for a portal, thought Sebastian. Although, this location was rather far off the beaten path. More so than usual. Not that that meant anything. There were likely many portals in extreme remote locations he had yet to find.

Problem was he didn't actually see a portal. If there were any in the vicinity, he should pick up on their frequency or shimmer. He should get something. Anything. At least, that's how he thought they worked.

A quick scan of the perimeter revealed a small, oval-shaped pond with a brook dribbling in from above. The hillside stretched up and away at a gentle grade. Nothing marked an ideal portal location, nothing but—

A notion struck him. It was slightly crazy, but he had nothing to lose. Why not, he figured. Sebastian took a deep breath and jumped into the pond. Hell, hope I'm right, he thought. He prayed his feet wouldn't collide with muddy ground in seconds.

Sebastian slipped through the water, the chill slicing straight through his clothing and biting into his skin. He dumped onto the hard ground below, connecting with a jolt. Sharp pain splintered up his shins, but otherwise he was fine. The jump had landed him in a hidden room below the water's surface. The water moved above, at the ceiling, and the moonlight filtered through, bathing him and the rest of the space in a soft, cool glow. Clearly magical, it had to have been created by the Gatekeepers.

"Where did you come from?"

Sebastian spun around at the sound of the man's voice. Only feet away stood a tall, broad, dark-haired man. He looked like an official Gatekeeper, for all Sebastian knew—although he was young, and that had to be a good thing. Sebastian had only met one other before.

Sebastian stood and bowed his head. "Didn't mean to startle you. I need to use your portal. You haven't made this one an easy find."

The Gatekeeper's face hardened. "This one isn't active yet, so it isn't resonating."

Sebastian bit his tongue. He wanted to laugh at his mistake, but knew it to be in bad form so he chose to behave. "I came because I was looking for you. I need your help."

The Gatekeeper turned his back on Sebastian and pretended to go back to work.

Sebastian approached him with caution. "Did I offend you? I didn't mean to. You are only the second Gatekeeper I've met. I should have shown better manners. My apologies."

The Gatekeeper's gaze flickered over Sebastian. "It is forgiven. Think nothing more of it. Now go, as this portal is not ready for you yet."

Sebastian dragged his hand along the wall of water. It was wet, yet firm. Oddly warm against his fingertips. "What is this place? How did you hold the water back, create this air pocket invisible from above?"

The Gatekeeper stopped what he was doing and a smug smile turned the corners of his lips. "Gatekeeper magic. It's not for you. It's only for my kind to know."

"Your kind. That's a lot of power for only one species to control, don't you think?"

"Look who's talking, Reaper."

"So you know what I am. That saves a bit of time and formality." Sebastian squared his shoulders, then placed his finger to his lips in a moment of thought. "Wouldn't it be nice to have a Reaper owe you a favor?"

The Gatekeeper's lips turned down into a frown. "How would that do me any good?"

Sebastian's eyes sparkled. "Are you kidding? Think about it."

The Gatekeeper nodded. "You may have a point. I can see there may be a benefit or two. What is it you want?"

Sebastian's insides buzzed, and he pushed down his anxiety over what he had to do next. "It should be rather easy. I need a couple of portals."

"I figured as much. Portals to where?"

"For starters, I need a quick one directly into Mobürn."

"There's a reason why there aren't any portals in or out of Mobürn. The dragons residing there want to be left alone. You are not dragon. They'll destroy you on sight."

"I'm very aware of the dangers. But this is a serious matter, and lives are hanging on a meat hook. Cut me some slack and help a Reaper out. What do you say? Will you or will you not help me?"

The Gatekeeper paced the small underwater room, his hand in constant motion, scratching through the back of his hair down to his neck. Tension emanated from him in thick, heavy waves, absorbing the oxygen, making the space almost unbearable.

Sebastian coughed into his hand, hoping to spur the conversation to a desired conclusion.

The Gatekeeper waved his finger like a nervous twitch. "If I do this for you, there will have to be a time limit. I can't leave the portal open indefinitely. Can you accomplish what you need to do within an hour's time?"

Sebastian's eyes widened. "One hour? To do everything? Find and talk to the individual I need, and get back or get stuck? Is that what you're saying?"

The Gatekeeper nodded.

"Looks like I don't have a choice. I agree to your terms." Sebastian put out his open hand.

The Gatekeeper sighed and narrowed his eyes on Sebastian. "There was more. What else did you want from me?"

"We can discuss that when and if I return from the first trip in one piece," Sebastian said. "Can we get started?"

"You mean now?"

"Is there any better time? I'd like to get going. Time is short, and I can't afford to waste any more."

The Gatekeeper shifted his weight and looked over Sebastian with an appraising eye. "I don't trust you."

"As you shouldn't."

"Why won't you tell me what else you seek?" He placed his hand on the tool harness at his side. The tool used to birth doorways to new realms and worlds.

Sebastian kicked his foot out, took a step. "Because, my new friend," his hand came down on the Gatekeeper's shoulder, "it may be a moot request, depending on how things play out in this first little adventure of mine."

The young Gatekeeper's eyes shifted over Sebastian, and then around the room. He appeared to look at everything, yet see nothing. His eyes were completely glazed over. "Okay."

Sebastian puckered his lips and drew back his brows. Watched while the Gatekeeper pulled the tool from his belt and began to draw a circle on the ground. Completed, he stepped to the side and tossed something from his hand across the divided space. He then chanted a few words Sebastian didn't understand.

The outer lines of the circle began to glow a brilliant orange and red, beaming through the dirt. Like fire breaking through the earth. At one point, the light ignited in hot white. It took off like the wick on a stick of dynamite, moving over the line until the whole circle burned brighter, more brilliantly than before. The portal burst to life, and then vanished. Sebastian knew the door was still there and had simply taken on its protective camouflage. He could feel the vibration, slight as it was, and knew exactly where to find the doorway.

The Gatekeeper turned to face Sebastian, no pride present in his demeanor. He looked concerned, rather than satisfied.

"Thank you…" Sebastian paused. "What do I call you?"

"I am Madoc."

"Thank you, Madoc. I owe you one." Sebastian shook the young Gatekeeper's hand, all the while his heart crammed up into his throat. Then he stepped forward and dropped through the portal.

11

BOLSVCK

Sebastian slipped through the portal, his hands grasping for the edge. He dangled in the air, an uneven terrain of rock and slow-flowing magma beneath him.

"Reap me," Sebastian mumbled.

Is this madness or pure genius in the portal placement? he wondered. It would be difficult for a dragon to accidently stumble through a door placed in the sky. Difficult for him to get back through, too.

Flinging his legs forward, Sebastian swung back and forth until constant momentum moved through his body, then released his hold. He flipped forward and landed on a large slab of slate. Volcanic matter slushed past in cracked veins running around and through the rocks. Quick jumps and skips had him moving across the rocks, using them as giant stepping-stones.

From stories—and a few directions from Zeke—Sebastian knew where to go. The dragons would gather in the sanctuary. The dragon Bolsvck—the mighty dragon who had refused to rule, the most feared and revered of all dragons, and Kyra's father—should be found there.

Marking the time on his watch, Sebastian moved at top speed through the canyon. What he was looking for had to be at a higher elevation, so his gaze traveled the walls in search of a path.

In canyons settled with dragons, there was no need for roads or paths. At least, not for Fire Dragons. They could fly to their destination. Sebastian would need to make his own path, but first he needed to identify his target. As he rounded the first bend, he saw a large, oversized-brick wall marked what he'd been looking for. He silently thanked Madoc for getting him so close. A short climb, and he was slipping into the dragons' damp lair. Barely in and the rock began to break, fall away beneath his feet. He slid down the embankment.

Dark, sharp claws slammed down at his feet, stopping him short. Sebastian had been expecting a Fire Dragon. Perhaps a scout or centennial. He never dreamed he'd run into a Black Dragon on this little errand. But here he was, fuming breath and all. Sebastian's mind spun with a whirlwind of information. He tried to remember what he'd read about them in all his species research. Research he'd done after meeting Kyra the first time. Black Dragons were dangerous, terribly vile. Possibly the most evil of the species.

Sleek, thin skin stretched ghastly over his skeleton structure, and his wings looked like moldy Swiss cheese. Vapors of fungal green seeped from the sides of his mouth, and the strong accompanying scent of rotting corpses burned Sebastian's nose hairs. From deeply sunken sockets, he stared down at Sebastian with blood-red eyes, and snarled.

The side of his lip quivered, lifting to show his all-too-sharp canines. "Your kind is not welcome here."

Sebastian's hands went up in peace and he bowed his head. "My apologies. I have come to beg an audience with Bolsvck."

Claws dragged immense scars through the earth. "Mighty Bolsvck does not lower to one such as you."

Sebastian glanced past the imposing dragon to the immense hole the cave opened up to. Muddy water ran through the center, dividing the cavern. On the far side sat a humongous red dragon with unique markings running the length of his body. His presence, majestic and commanding. The largest Fire Dragon Sebastian had ever imagined. He had to be Bolsvck. He wasn't alone, though. Dragons of all shapes, sizes, and colors moved throughout the sanctuary. The interior of the mountain was a bustling dragon community. Kyra hadn't lied when she'd said the stories of dragon extinction were greatly exaggerated.

Light poured in on the hollow from a break in the ceiling. It glimmered off Boslvck's hide, marking him for the treasure he was, a born leader of his kind. Near his front leg, up by the stretch of his neck, shining in the summer's light, was a Dragon King's marking. Sebastian watched him use his fire to warm the ground and then cozy into a position on a high rock overlooking his flock—or dignity, as it were in this case.

Sebastian glanced at the Black Dragon, then back to Kyra's father. "But I just need—" He took a step toward his goal, toward Bolsvck. A black arm swept down, claws extended. It hit Sebastian hard and fast. Knocked him off his feet and sent him flying backwards.

Sebastian crashed into the mountain's rock side. Splinters of pain shot out across his backside. A boil of hot, white pain ruptured his gut. Sebastian doubled over, threw his hands on his knees for support. Air—need air. He pounded a fist to his chest, and his windpipe opened with a massive gasp. "What the hell?" Sebastian stumbled forward. "I promise you, Bolsvck will want to hear what I have to say."

"Tell me. I'll be the judge." Smaller and brilliantly bright, a White Dragon stepped from around the corner. She pinned her sharp gaze directly on Sebastian. She might've resembled an ice carving, but Sebastian wouldn't be fooled. Supreme intelligence dwelled in the dragon's eyes. Sebastian would have to watch what he said and did, or he'd wind up dead—maybe.

The Black Dragon hissed, turned, and swept his tail wide. Sebastian jumped, the massive tail brushing past him far too close for comfort. He narrowly escaped the force of another hit or smack against the rocks. Earth shook, bringing small rocks crumbling from above, and the Black Dragon stormed away.

The White Dragon lowered her head and narrowed her gaze. "Do not keep me waiting, little creature. Out with it."

Sebastian cared for this dragon even less. She may be smaller, less intimidating in size and appearance, but there was a cunning about her that bordered on terrifying. Sebastian glanced at his watch. The portal would be closing soon. He had to hurry. "No chance of seeing Bolsvck?"

She straightened her neck, raising her head high. "None."

Sebastian let out a sigh. "You must make sure he gets this message. Dragons are being slaughtered upland, and his daughter Kyra may be in danger."

"His daughter is dead to us."

Sebastian blinked, his body jolting in response to her reaction. He refused to believe Bolsvck felt that way. "I fear the dragons being killed aren't random killings, but part of a bigger plan. I thought he should be aware."

The White Dragon opened one eye wider. White light shimmered around her and a woman suddenly stood before Sebastian. Her skin was pale, hairless, and covered in white scrolled markings. "And human forms of the dragons are being found?"

Sebastian nodded. "How did you know?"

She acted as if Sebastian hadn't spoken. "You were brave to come here and bring Bolsvck the news. I thank you on his behalf." She bowed her head, and Sebastian returned the gesture. Then she pointed him toward the exit. To appease her, Sebastian pretended to leave.

The compass spun, showing him the way. The watch in his palm told him he had twenty-five minutes until the portal closed. Was it enough time? Probably not, but he had to try.

No dragons had followed him out. He slipped the folded piece of paper from Talia out of his pocket and read the instructions. Get the dagger, she'd said. No doubt an impossible task. He should have asked for a portal to the dagger's front door. Sebastian studied the diagram, and when he felt confident he knew it by heart, he slipped the paper back in his pocket and crept into the cave again.

There had to be a better approach. This time Sebastian would find it, use it. Reapers must have cool superpowers he wasn't aware of. Maybe he could go invisible. He thought on that. Didn't do any good if he didn't know how to make it work. All he knew how to do was reap, and he sure as hell wasn't going to reap any dragons. Not if he wanted Kyra's father on his side. Question was, what was he doing associating with so many terrible and unstable monsters?

Keeping to the shadows, he crept as quick as he could, following the map now inked in his memory. He wasn't a hundred percent certain what the dagger was for, but if he understood the directions clearly, it would help retrieve Kyra's dragon, and that's all that mattered right now. He was getting the damn thing, at any cost.

Sebastian slipped around the corner and came face to face with the White Dragon. Orange eyes flickered, nostrils flared. Sebastian ventured a guess she wasn't happy with his change in direction.

"Didn't I show you the way out?" Her claws extended and began to tap.

Decision time. What was his defense move if he was avoiding the reap? "Well, yes," he said, vying for time. "Then I realized I forgot something." He reached down in his soul and pulled. Dug into hers, sifting, searching.

"And what was that?" She stepped forward, baring her teeth.

"This," Sebastian said with a snap of his fingers.

The White Dragon threw her head to the ceiling and roared. Sebastian hadn't known what to expect, never having dealt with a dragon in this way before. Wasn't even sure if dragons had nightmares, any fears, he could pluck. But there it was, prancing around at the front of her gray matter, waiting for Sebastian to swoop in and play. And play he did. He kicked opened doors, knocked down walls, and threw off unwieldy camouflage meant to hide and contain the dragon's deepest secrets. Her inadmissible horrors.

A massive White Dragon with a mean scar across his brow leaped through the rubble of a toppled memory wall. It was only a recollection, and he didn't see Sebastian, didn't engage. He roared at the tiny dragonling cowering in the far corner of the host dragon's mind. Anger rippled his hide, wiping his tail, and spewing smoke from his nostrils. The dragonling wailed, and then the image evaporated, only to be replaced with another.

This one slammed into Sebastian, knocking him to his trance-state butt and shaking his Mara nightmare hold. The state of retrospection shuddered, leaving Sebastian struggling to maintain control. The source of the interference—a ginormous, iridescent red dragon. He spread his wings and flapped. His voice exploded in a blast of defending command. Legends crumbled and fell before him. Like a changeling, the beast's face fluctuated, beating back and forth like the thrum of his mighty tail, between the dragon and the man Sebastian recognized as Marcus. Only, Sebastian felt not a single drop of mercy in the man's soul. He hadn't detected such ugliness in Marcus's person. Sebastian hated him, plain and true.

Hellhounds and chaos monsters flanked Marcus's side, rushed, battered, and destroyed everything in their path. An army of zilants flew above, his to command. The winged, snake-like creatures hissed and wiggled, creating the impression of a slithering sky. Sebastian wondered how Marcus had managed to align all the lower demons. Or why he would want to.

Then Marcus yelled, a mighty bellow, and the zilants dove into the crowd of cowering dragons already under siege by hellhounds and chaos demons. Screams fractured the memory, knocked Sebastian clear. He'd only recently become aware of Marcus's dragon status. Now he'd learned of all the evil Marcus could control at the tip of his claw. Sebastian jerked, shook his head and the thoughts clear.

The White Dragon's nightmares had been enlightening, and Sebastian was now concerned beyond any Mara's nightmare illusion for Kyra. If Marcus had any army behind him this time, dragons could soon become Reaper business. Some really nasty dragons already feared Marcus. What did that mean for Kyra?

The dragon in front of him clawed at the ground, swung her body from side to side, and screeched at such a massive volume the sound bounced off the tunnel walls and set Sebastian's ears to ringing. He ran from the site as quick as he could. Ran before more dragons came to her aid and caught him in the process.

The thunder of their approach rattled the tunnels, the noise deafening as more dragons joined in the howling, rocks and sediment falling from walls all around him. Talia's map led him to a room not far from his run-in with the White Dragon. It wasn't much of a space. Round, no windows, only one entrance. What made it special, worth the trouble to visit, was the treasure it stored. Pure gold lined the walls in piles. Jewels, statues, goblets, and so much more. A dragon's hoard stored in the cavern, and on a pillar set high in the center was a shiny dagger, the handle simple, the blade set long with a curve. But he knew it was the one he needed, so he set toward it in a run.

Full speed in his stride, he hit the column and jumped. As soon as his hand wrapped around the dagger's hilt, he felt it. Incredible power. He knew why the dragons kept the weapon hidden away. It was dangerous to them, strong beasts as they were. He pulled the blade up against his chest and dove down against the column's base, back pressed to its cold surface.

"It's gone!" a voice cried out.

Sebastian crouched down and peeked around the side of the column. Thankfully he'd landed on the back side, not visible from the entrance. A small, youthful Fire Dragon stood in the doorway. He marched in, galloped around and sniffed the air, then marched out again. "Nothing. I got nothing. Must be gone."

Curious. Sebastian wondered why the young dragonet couldn't smell him. Not that there was time to worry about it. Dragons yelled and thumped in the tunnel outside. Sebastian glanced at his watch. Eleven minutes. He wasn't going to make it. He looked down at the dagger and thought of Kyra. Thought of Marcus and what he would do to Kyra. Sebastian zipped around the column, rushed for the tunnel and the portal waiting outside.

"Where did you come fro—?" The young Fire Dragon never got to finish his question. Sebastian had him flailing on the ground within seconds, squirming in fear of being pulverized by a gnarly Black Dragon.

Sebastian wiped the sweat from his brow. At the moment, he was thankful for his Mara talents, even if he didn't condone the use of them. He looked away from the young dragon pitching to the fever of his own nightmare.

Dragons now came at him so quickly it was like they were

seeping out of the walls. He couldn't grab their fears and fling them back fast enough. Nor could he run fast enough. He dodged left, and then right, slid under the belly of one and realized that wasn't going to work. His plan was flawed.

He pulled out the dagger, ran with it in his grasp.

Smaller dragons backed away, slipped behind and followed from the rear. But the larger beasties were not so easily intimidated.

Darkness swam, swirled in Sebastian's belly. It ripped up his esophagus and exploded through the tunnels as he moved for the exit. Dragons fell away.

No!

Sebastian clamped his mouth shut. He hadn't meant to throw extinction at their souls. Never meant to cause them any pain, much less something worse. He glanced behind him. Dragons stammered, some collapsed, but none were dead. Thank the Reaper, none were dead. Sebastian put the wind at his back and ran faster. Ran with all that he was and all that he had. Ran because Kyra's life depended upon it.

They were roaring, screaming, howling behind him. He knew they came, but he dared not look back. Over the wall he went. Across the dust trail and slate rocks until he was leaping with as much spring as he could muster.

Sebastian swung through the portal not a minute too soon. It collapsed in on itself moments after he successfully pulled through to the other side.

"I didn't think you were going to make it," Madoc said. "Where to next?"

*****

Knuckles scratched and bruised, Sebastian raised his hand to knock on the door. He should have worn fingerless gloves, hidden the damage so as not to alarm Kyra. Too late now. He knocked three times. The door swung open almost immediately.

Kyra stood before him, binder in her arms. The binder toppled to the ground.

"Oh my God!" She grabbed him and pulled him into the apartment, closing the door behind them. "I thought you stood me up." Her hands wandered his face, traced a long line above his brow. It stung, and he flinched. How bad did he look? He hadn't thought to look in a mirror. She pushed him deeper into the apartment and Sebastian hesitated, felt Marcus's barrier keeping him out, then Talia's charm working brilliantly. Sebastian stepped beyond the boundary with only the slightest of resistance. Kyra led him to the sofa and pushed him down, then ran back to the bedroom.

"When she said..." Sebastian mumbled, and looked from the dinette table to the counter and every other flat surface in the room, never finishing his thought. Sunflower arrangements adorned every logical space. He felt a smile tugging at his lip, then worry dropped it into a frown. She'd said she kept the flowers because of their suggestion of warmth. Why was she so cold? That's what he needed to figure out.

He studied the mess of work papers spread out on the coffee table. Noticed the highball glass half-full sitting in a ring of condensation among the disorder. She was working from home—and drinking. He leaned forward, took a whiff. Wowza! Strong stuff. His body jerked up and away. Instinctively, his hand reached for the small vial of Spiritual Peace he was carrying with him. His skin itched. He wanted to take a sip now. He moved his hand away from the tiny bottle.

With a sigh, he relaxed back into the cushions of the sofa. Foot tapping, fingers drumming against his thigh, he was anxious to be moving. Dammit if he wasn't already messing things up in her presence. He should have grabbed her and left. She'd caught him off guard with her greeting, laying her hands on him the way she did. He liked it. Far more than he could put into words.

"Hell," he mumbled, and dropped his head into his hands.

"What's that?"

Kyra was back. She threw herself down next to him on the sofa, flipping to face him. Their legs pressed firmly against one another. Marcus would erupt like a volcano if he were to walk in. In her hand she held a damp washcloth, and she began to dab at his forehead.

"Is it bad?" he asked.

"You haven't seen it?"

Sebastian shook his head.

"You should clean up okay. What happened?"

"Nothing you need to worry about." He watched her mouth while she applied ointment to his temple, followed by a bandage. She was stunning, so intoxicating; he didn't want to drag his gaze away. Yet it wasn't long before he found himself searching her neckline, looking for the dragon tooth Talia kept telling him to locate. Kyra used to wear the trinket on a string around her neck. Where was it now?

When she'd finished playing nurse, she leaned in and kissed her completed work. Sebastian closed his eyes and savored the moment.

"Oh, I'm sorry," Kyra said. "Did I go too far?"

Sebastian opened his eyes and looked at her. His brows felt heavy, weighted with concern for her comment. They pressed into his eyes. "What do you mean?"

"I thought we'd done that before. It felt right. Was I wrong?"

Sebastian continued to stare at her, his confusion still clouded.

"The kiss. Haven't we kissed before?"

His chest expanded, filling with air and understanding. Was she acting on feelings without actual knowledge? Or was she recalling the kiss she'd planted on him that night in his tarot card trailer? Either way, it gave him hope. Hope that she returned his feelings.

A small smile cracked his face. "We haven't kissed before. It doesn't mean I am opposed to it." He'd lied. But he wasn't going to count their one and only kiss to date. Not under these circumstances. And he wasn't going to take advantage. He would win her soul over in such a way that she'd love him for all eternity. Memory return or not. That was the hope, at least.

Kyra bit the inside of her lip and studied him. Pain, want, desire: it all moved through him as he looked back at her. Never had they been so close, and yet felt so far. One mistake, and all possibilities for the future could shatter.

He sat back against the sofa. They should go—he knew they should go—but he didn't want to end whatever was happening between them. The edge of his thumb caressed the soft skin of her cheek. "Are you okay? Did he hurt you in any way?" His gaze wandered to her glass of liquid fire on the table.

Following his look, she shook her head and turned closer to him. They aligned, Kyra shifting until they were perfectly positioned, parallel to each other. Staring at her lips, he feared making a move and losing her forever. Then again, he feared not making a move and losing her forever.

She leaned in and pressed her lips to his. Soft, like silk gliding over smooth, bare skin. She was spring in the winter. Her lips curved to his, then melted around them. The sweet, delicious taste of nectarines. It was unexpected and never more welcome.

Kyra slid back and gazed at Sebastian. "You're saying we've never done that before?"

His hands slipped from her face and glided down her arm, stopping above her elbow. "Not like that."

"Felt like a perfect fit."

Sebastian's gaze lowered. The kiss did feel perfect, yet he didn't feel right about it. As long as she didn't remember who she was, he would never feel right. His gut tied into a knot. She would be lost to him when she finally remembered. Remembered he took advantage. That dragon anger of hers would take over and she would hate him.

As gently as he knew how, he moved her to the side. "I'm sorry, Kyra. I never should have kissed you. Not while you're missing your memories."

"You didn't kiss me. I kissed you."

"But I shouldn't have allowed it. You may hate me later." Sebastian dragged his fingers through his hair, let his gaze wander toward the front door. "What of Marcus?"

Kyra slapped her hands in her lap. "Something's not right with Marcus."

Yes! Thank the dragon gods. She finally sees it.

A loud snore burst from the other room, the bedroom. Sebastian stared at Kyra, his eyes wide with questions.

Her lips tightened, held back a laugh. "Chet." She giggled. "We're supposed to be working. He can't handle his liquor." She pointed to an almost-empty glass on the bar separating the room from the kitchen. "I get so tired of being watched all the time." She rolled her eyes.

Sebastian was proud of her, but didn't want to hang around a second longer, tempting fate. As much as he loved sitting here with Kyra and had wanted the kiss to last for endless hours, there was someplace they needed to be. And Chet was a serious mood killer.

He clasped his hand around hers. "Listen. I'm going to ask something of you, and it may sound strange. Crazy, even. Will you trust me?"

Kyra's eyes widened, looked excited. "What do I have to do?"

12

SACRIFICE

Essence of Anodynse, incense extracted from the spinal fluid of dragons, wrapped around Marcus. It created a thick magical cloud, crisscrossing his body. Marcus knelt before the flames built upon sacred stones from the temple of Rajūn, the first dragon and great water deity.

With slow, deliberate movements, Marcus directed the vapors toward himself. He inhaled and sniffed them. Absorbed them through his naked skin. He came before the bearer of dragons a clean slate. Sweat glistened over the curves of his physique, droplets falling from his body in trickles. Leila moved around the perimeter, fanning the outlying flames, and temperatures rose.

Tossing and thrashing in their jars of effervescing energy, the dragons of sacrifice sat arranged on the floor of the Great Hall in a diamond around Marcus. Kyra's dragon represented water and fire. She had been placed center, directly before him. To the left, in a mesh of mossy glimmer, was a forest giant—a Green Dragon. To the right, trapped in a brilliant display of illumination, the shrewd ice beast. Behind him, a slightly too docile mountain dweller, and at front point, ears frilled, horn scraping at the glass, a vain Blue Dragon hissed and chomped.

Marcus warmed with confidence. Nothing could stop him now. Soon he'd absorb every one of those dragons within his soul, and be more powerful than any dragon to ever exist. Never again would the dragon council be able to banish him.

His skin tightened across his chest. He laughed out loud as fire and fumes consumed him, his own dragon sliding in, returning from purgatory. His beast reeked of death and decay. Didn't bother Marcus one bit. His heart was dark, and he liked it that way.

"Keep chanting!" Leila scolded. "Your beast is not secure until the chant is complete."

Marcus shot her a stern look, but followed her demands. His chest burned. Possibly with anger. He wasn't used to people telling him what to do. She was the first in a great while to even try.

Leila came to the fire with a knife bearing the markings of his family crest. She tilted it at an angle so he could verify its authenticity.

He laid out his arms palms up, hands curled into fists, and then gritted his teeth in preparation for what came next. Leila cut matching marks into each arm using the tip of the blade. When completed, the cuts looked like eyes with a line running through them. Blood ran from the newly cut slashes and small brass bowls on the floor below caught the runoff.

With the matching eyes of Rajūn cut into his arms, Marcus opened his arms wide to receive. Leila moved to his bare chest and pressed the point of the knife to the place just above his heart. His heart stopped, his chant paused, and his eyes flickered down to her. She stood so close. Nothing could stop her from plunging the blade deep into his soul. She tilted her head up to meet his gaze and smiled gingerly, as if she'd heard his thoughts.

His insides burned. A fury of hatred for her whirled out of control, the control she exhibited over him the accelerant. Yet, he feared her. For that reason she would have to die. Not yet, though. After he got what he wanted.

She smiled at him and he didn't trust it, didn't trust her. The smile was too knowledgeable, too deceitful. The knife tip stung. Sliced through his skin with the burn of a wild flame. He didn't look down. Instead, he kept his gaze steady on her and savored the singe.

Every sense heightened, making him acutely aware of each

breath, every change taking place around him, within the room. He closed his eyes and concentrated. Leila's body heat changed and she shuffled away from him. Marcus picked up on her subtle vibrations moving through the old tile floor. She was walking backwards, toward the first of the dragons. Why was she trying to be so quiet? Was she double-crossing him? Trying to inhibit his ability to follow through?

If so, he would finish it. He would finish her. He'd been born for finalities.

Leila uncapped the first jar. The lid sprang free and the monstrous Forest Dragon jumped out onto the jar's edge, both beast and her majestic power bursting free like a sandstorm bursting through a once-closed door. She released a resounding war cry as the magical energy, disguised as a euphoric light show, swirled up out of its prison and across the room toward Marcus. Like dust pulled to the vacuum, the dragon's magic drew straight into Marcus's body through the cut on his arm.

Marcus reeled backwards, the force slamming into him like a full-grown gargoyle. Power surged through his arms, lightning quick into his bloodstream, the desire to tear a giant hole in a mountain's side a new and exciting prospect.

The sound of another jar opening, the cap hitting the hard ground, froze Marcus's arteries, and ice crusted his bones. The power of the Ice Dragon had entered his system through the symbol cut in his other arm. The floor came up to meet him, his hands slamming flat onto the filthy tile. His upper torso was weighted down, thrown out of balance with the rest of him.

His muscles strained, his jaw locked, and he pushed himself up. He refused to show weakness. Weakness was for the inferior. Leila might as well have put a torch to his ears, for the way they felt. They could have been turning to ash by the moment, they burned with such intensity. He tilted them to the ceiling.

A minor shift in the environment had occurred. One not likely detectible by any creature, human or otherwise. Yet he felt it, if barely. Then he saw it—a portal.

"Hurry," he growled.

Leila glanced behind her at the shimmering air a moment before it snapped straight and disappeared. She ripped the top of the third jar open and dashed around the diamond to the fourth, releasing both giants almost simultaneously. The dragon essences came at him from opposite directions, colliding into the marks cut deep in his chest. Magic misted around Marcus and the stones with the forceful fumes of a dragon-induced bonfire.

His goal was almost actualized. One more to go. Absorb the magical life force of each dragon. Power and rage coursed through his blood, his bones, his everything.

Sebastian and Kyra slipped out of the portal and collapsed onto the floor of the Great Hall.

Marcus's gaze narrowed in on Kyra. His heart remained steady and his mind started calculating. The little carnie had messed everything up, bringing her here. She was supposed to be his. He had the perfect little Bronze Dragon picked out to tame her.

Leila ripped open the final glass prison, releasing Kyra's dragon, Kalrapura. Orange flecks of light floated up into the air, up between Marcus and Kyra, and Marcus envisioned Kyra as the dragon who had pulled him from the water the day he'd first found her. That dragon, that Moorigad, would now be his.

"Marcus!" Kyra screamed. "What are you doing?"

Leila moved a step closer to him. "Don't get distracted. Keep the ritual flowing."

Sebastian lurched forward and pointed at Leila. "You! You're helping him?"

Kyra and Sebastian had their hands linked together. Kyra now grabbed his arm and pulled close to his ear. "You know her?"

"Only from a dream," Sebastian said. Kyra started to pull away from him, but Sebastian clutched onto her and held tight. "It's nothing, Kyra. I'll explain later."

Marcus's skin was scorching. The more he watched Kyra with the idiot carnie, the more it throbbed. He'd have to obliterate the boy now. He was too much of a liability. Always getting in the way. Or...he could consume Sebastian, like he had so many demons in the past. Yes. Consume him and take within him the power of a

Mara. A wayward grin twitched at the edge of Marcus's lips.

Then unmatched power slammed Marcus in the chest, knocking him off his feet. He laughed and laid his head on the ground. Every part of him tingled, dancing to life on a new level of awareness. Never had he felt so incredible, and he had Kyra to thank for it. Wicked delight curled at the edges of his lips, and he was only halfway through the ritual. It was only going to get better.

Five dragons, and all their magic and power, were his. Now miniature versions of what the beasts once were flew in complete disarray above him. They were nothing more than vessels for the dragons' spirits: their vitality, their hearts, their liveliness. Soon, even those would belong to Marcus.

Sebastian scrambled to the side. Marcus saw him coming, knew what he was up to. Sebastian lurched for Kyra's dragon and Marcus roared. The walls vibrated. Marcus flexed and morphed in a fraction of a second. It felt like someone had shoved a steel-toed boot far up his ass and pulled his intestinal tract out. Excruciating, but he got a tail out of the process, and he swept it across the room, sending Sebastian airborne. He creamed into the far wall. Fell in a heap on the floor.

Kyra screamed.

Leila laughed.

And the sacrificial dragons, now void of their magical core, took flight, screeching objections that echoed throughout the hall.

Sebastian pushed himself into a sitting position. "You captured each of the dragons' essences?"

Marcus sneered, didn't answer, and then began to bulge and bubble all over his body. His intestines were boiling. The process was cooking him from the inside. Bloody shit, he cursed silently. Then peace washed over him. He was dragon—sort of. A deformed mutation of a dragon. Not for long, though. He would fix that.

He stretched his long neck high in the air. Then—snap! He chomped down on the Ice Dragon. Caught her mid-flight. He devoured her slowly. Allowed himself the satisfaction of enjoying every tingle and twinge gained from the beast's life force. He was drunk on her power, so drunk he could sleep for days. Of course he wouldn't. There were four more dragons on the menu.

The remaining dragons flew in a defensive form of chaos, their cries bouncing off the walls of the old party hall. Spotting two dragons clinging close together, Marcus lumbered toward them. They separated. He pitched to the side, caught the Green Dragon by the wing. Flipping her around, he tossed her up and caught her as she pitched back down.

As before, his power surged and his desire to nap increased.

Three more to go.

And it continued. The mountain dweller, the horned Blue Dragon. Marcus devoured them both.

Kyra crouched in the corner, screaming, spewing words of hate and loathing. He didn't care. He'd fix her later. Sebastian stood, brushed the dirt off, and looked a lot like a thorn in Marcus's claw. Damn boy didn't know when to give up. Silly, he even had himself a toy dagger. As if that would help. Marcus roared with laughter.

Kid couldn't do anything. Marcus had one dragon left to go. Kyra's dragon, the prized Moorigad. He'd saved the best for last.

Sebastian grabbed Kyra, pulling her from Marcus's reach. "Do you trust me?" he yelled.

"You know the answer to that," Kyra answered.

"There's no room for doubt."

Marcus roared. He hated talk of trust between Kyra and Sebastian. He hated Sebastian.

Kyra's eyes grew wide, and she stared at Marcus, then nodded to Sebastian.

Sebastian grabbed something from the back of his jacket. Marcus lumbered closer and watched Sebastian press what looked like the dagger against Kyra's skin. Red spread from the spot as Sebastian sliced a line into Kyra's forearm.

"Ouch!" she yelled, and grabbed her arm.

Kyra's dragon shrieked, turned, and looked toward the carnie pair. Kalrapura suddenly moved at an alarming speed in their direction. Marcus chomped down where she had been, but she was gone.

A tiny sound escaped Kyra's lips and she began to shuffle backwards, her stare glued on the dragon diving directly at her. She tripped and fell into Sebastian's arms. The dagger clamored against the tile floor.

They were not allowed to ruin this for him. Marcus pinned his sights on Sebastian and hurled into him with all his rage at the helm. He wanted blood, and the Mara bastard's suited him perfectly fine. The blow knocked Kyra sideways, hurtling her into a heap on the floor. Sebastian yelled for her and whipped the dagger out from his side, where it had fallen moments ago.

Too frantic? Panicked? The Mara boy accidently cut himself on the leg, pulling the dagger free. Blood dripped down Sebastian's calf. A victorious grin was already spreading across Marcus's face. Careless mistakes would make him an easy kill.

Behind Marcus, Leila danced in a circle. A circle of insanity. He would crush her sooner rather than later, Marcus decided.

Sebastian swung the dagger at Marcus. The blade barely grazed him, yet he burned with the fires of a thousand Hells. Marcus let out a roar of a Dragon King magnified to the power of twenty. The walls shook, crumbling dirt from its old stucco. Bits of the ceiling cracked, broke free, and plummeted.

Kyra collapsed on her knees and hugged herself, favoring her head. She was like a wounded animal, and Marcus savored the vision. Then she was scrambling across the littered floor and pulling at Sebastian's wound.

Sebastian grabbed Kyra's wrist and pulled her to her feet. She wavered. Marcus's upper lip pulled back, exposed his sharp canines. He was ready to devour, and devour he would.

Sebastian glanced around the hall, then over Kyra. Marcus knew what the boy was doing. Stupid boy was looking for Kyra's dragon. He still thought he could save her. Marcus roared with laughter, and he saw Kyra's eyes glaze over. Marcus roared again, and this time the air trembled. Orange specks shimmered, floated around Kyra and Sebastian, and Marcus's howl only grew louder and more intense.

A shock wave exploded around them, and Sebastian and

Kyra, even the ginormous dragon that was Marcus, were knocked off their feet. Marcus lay in a heap as tingles of energy seeped out from every place a cut had been on his body. Orange, gold, and slight flecks of blue oozed from his dragon husk in a surge of magical, churning dust. In a whirling dash, it moved across the hall and disappeared in the explosive shock wave around Sebastian and Kyra.

Marcus's claws dug chunks out of the ground. He growled, then rushed at Sebastian, his eyes ablaze with plans for his ingestion. He was getting Kyra's dragon one way or another. If he had to eat both of them to get it, so be it!

Whoosh. The portal oscillated.

A rush of air flew into the hall, slammed into Marcus, threw him to the ground. Marcus couldn't believe his eyes. He was staring up at Bolsvck, eyes burning with fury, nostrils flared and ready to burn. What would possibly bring Bolsvck here now? Unless the Dragon Elders had finally recognized Marcus's potential.

Marcus's chest puffed out and shoulders squared, then he was tumbling backwards, slammed in the breast by Bolsvck's wrecking ball tail. Marcus lunged back, missed his mark, and chomped on air. A wing the size of a small building knocked Marcus sideways. Didn't matter. He would still win this. He was confident. After all, Bolsvck was a dragon of legend, which meant he was old. Marcus still had strength and youth on his side.

Still, Bolsvck was big! And he blocked Marcus's clear line of attack at Sebastian, or capture of Kyra. Bolsvck stood with his wings spread wide in clear protection of his daughter beyond.

Marcus thrashed at the ground and roared, then watched the punk Sebastian take his girl back through the portal. There was nothing he could do to stop him. Not with Bolsvck standing in the way. Marcus bellowed. He would kill them for this. Kill them all. Fired with anger and frustration, Marcus swung his powerful tail, slammed it into the sidewall. Drywall and concrete cracked and shattered, and debris splattered across the room. He lunged at Bolsvck, jaws chomping.

Muscles bound with fire and fury, the two dragons twisted

and spun in a heated battle of strength and cunning. Marcus's confidence led the fight, but Bolsvck was a hardier opponent than he had anticipated. Plus, tingles and sparks continued to nip at his body, along the incisions meant to pull in and trap the power of additional magical beings. Marcus clobbered Bolsvck once in the side, but staggered from the weight of his own blow. Had he lost something? Had one of the sacrificial dragons somehow escaped?

His head swooned and he struck out, forcing Bolsvck to keep his distance. Marcus's breath came in long, labored efforts.

"Give it up, Balidhug. You cannot best me," Bolsvck sneered. "You made a mistake trying to take power again. You should have stayed wherever you were. Remained quiet. We would have left you alone."

"What do you know?" Marcus yelled. "You are stuck in your old ways. You won't even lead, but the people, the dragons, need a leader. I will be that leader."

Bolsvck huffed, lumbered in a slow circle around Marcus. Marcus searched the area, every dark corner, for Leila. He saw no sign of her. Damn that Mara bitch for bolting when I could use her most, Marcus hissed internally.

"You cannot rule by way of destruction," Bolsvck said.

Marcus let the words slide in one ear and straight out the other. There wasn't a thing Bolsvck could say Marcus wanted to hear.

"You only live because I allowed it, nephew. You'd be wise to heed me now."

Except maybe that.

Marcus's head snapped forward, his nostrils flared, eyes blazed wide. "I am not your kin!"

"Are you not? Are you so certain of your truth?"

Marcus shook his head back and forth and back and forth. He would not believe. He was no descendant of the wretched royal family. Claws flared, razor-sharp, he lashed out, pulling flesh from Bolsvck's face.

Everything around them erupted in chaos and noise. The thunder of Bolsvck's uproar. Bolsvck's fire consuming all oxygen.

The walls crumbling and falling. And the hulk of a talon slapping Marcus across the Great Hall. The last thing Marcus saw, before his heavy eyelids succumbed, was Leila peering down at him.

13

ERRONEOUS

Sebastian and Kyra rushed from the portal, their shoes slipping on the damp grass. Arcs of silver tinsel glistened in the moonlight, remnants from the sprinklers having run only moments earlier. Kyra caught a mud patch and slid. Sebastian's arm shot out and steadied her.

The surrounding city assaulted him, attacked with thoughts and memories Sebastian was too weak to combat. He pulled the tiny vial of Talia's Spiritual Peace from his pocket, took a swig. It was like a warm rinse gliding over his brain. The nagging, the internal chatter stopped.

They had arrived in the city park, the final location Madoc had set up a portal for Sebastian. He owed the Gatekeeper big for all that he had done. The passage behind them quivered and snapped shut, just as he had been told it would. No one could follow them now.

Sebastian released a deep breath in relief. The night air around them chilled his sweat-coated skin. Things may have turned out alright, but it didn't stop him from stressing in the process. He looked over at Kyra. She was watching him.

"What the hell was all that?" Kyra burst both in words and body language, her arms flailing and swinging around, attempting to pinpoint the portal.

Sebastian shifted his weight and studied her. There was a change in her. He wondered... "That was your boyfriend, up to no good. You saw that, right?"

"He was trying to eat my dragon!"

Sebastian jolted. Inside, he was a mass of exploding fireworks. "You remember your dragon? What else do you remember?"

She shook her head and gazed at the grass off to the side. "I don't know. It's all kind of hazy." She looked back at Sebastian. "Was that my dad?"

"Yeah, I think it was." Sebastian's lips curled into a crooked grin.

"Don't move!"

Sebastian and Kyra snapped their heads to the side. They were surrounded by what looked like soldiers. Sebastian recognized the way they were dressed. They looked a lot like the group who had rescued him previously. His chest fluttered and confusion flooded his brain. "What—?"

"Quiet! You weren't given permission to speak."

Someone whacked him in the back of the head with the butt of their rifle. The waves of pain rolled through his skull like an earthquake. He spun around and reached for the gun. Tense pain punched through his chest. He slipped and sank to the ground, landing on the wet grass. His whole body exploded with electric pain. He fought against it, wanted to stand up and fight, but couldn't find the strength. Wires carrying the powerful current clung to the front of him. They lit him up like the carnival fun zone and it hurt like a son-of-a-monster.

Somewhere Kyra was yelling, but he couldn't see her. There was a barrage of shouts and yells. Too many shots being fired.

A man lowered his face to Sebastian's. His eyes were dull and lacked the spark of life, but Sebastian recalled him immediately, having seen his mug earlier in the day—in a family portrait. He was Jon Davies, father to Sophie and Alice. This was bad. Extremely bad.

Alice's father narrowed his gaze directly in on Sebastian. It was commanding, hard. "You are wanted for the murder of Officer Alice Sullivan and Lieutenant Byran Crane."

Sebastian balked. "You've got it all wrong." He tried to respond. Tried to lift his arm, felt his hands sear with flame.

"No," Jon Davies said. "You got it wrong when you decided to visit my home." He leaned into Sebastian's space, and Sebastian tried to melt into the ground beneath him. "You made an even bigger mistake when you kept Alice's locket as a kill souvenir."

Sebastian didn't even have to reach into his pocket. At the mere mention of the locket, he could feel the weight of it. It pulled at him, wanted to drown him in a forever sea of guilt and sorrow. Damn Reapers. Damn Maras, too. He hated them all. Hated himself for being either, and for being both. "Tell your wife I'm sorry."

Davies narrowed his stare at Sebastian. The walkie clipped to his belt squawked. Static and hum came to life and announced a flurry of activity at Club Afterlife. Balidhug's men were on the move. Davies grunted. "He can't hide from us. Moves again, we'll find him. Now we have you." He pushed a foot against Sebastian's shoulder and rocked him. "You working with the beast, boy?"

"Me? Work with Marcus?"

Yells, then screams, erupted on their right. A deafening roar quaked through the park trees. Men and women flew past them overhead. His accuser looked up, his face widening, eyes bulging. His brow narrowed, his gaze flooding in confusion. Poor guy couldn't grasp what was happening. Not yet. Sebastian knew. He knew exactly what was going on. Then Davies was gone, knocked away by a large orange tail. Kyra the dragon appeared before him in full water form. She scooped Sebastian up and took off into the night.

Funny how things could end up. It had started with Kyra, the girl who held his heart, rescuing another in a similar manner— sort of. Now it was him she held, and they ran from the people who wanted to destroy the man she'd previously rescued, and who now wanted him dead as well. His life was completely messed up, but at least he had Kyra. For now, anyway.

Or did he?

He bobbed up and down on the shoulder of the big orange beast, feeling woozy. Damn electrocution, damn organized movement, and damn two Kyras.

Wait. Sebastian rubbed his head. Why were there two Kyras?

He narrowed his eyes, stared at the girl running behind them. "Kyra?"

"Slow down, Mom. You're moving too fast."

Mom! What? He'd gone to see her father and failed. How had her mother gotten here? Sebastian tried to turn, get a better look at the dragon holding him. He slipped. Everything went black.

*****

Sebastian's eyes sprang open, his body already bounding off the bed. "Kyra?"

Chelsea's hand pressed against his chest and pushed him back to the bed. "She's fine. She's outside arguing with her mother." Chelsea rolled her eyes. "You, sir," she shoved her pointer finger at him, "shouldn't move so fast. You've had a tough time of it recently."

Sebastian shook the fatigue off. He felt fine. Taking a mental inventory of his faculties, he really did feel good. Interesting, considering what he'd recently been through. "I'm fine, Chelsea." He grabbed her hand, then paused. Stared at her, searching her eyes.

She pulled away, looked away. "Something wrong?"

"No." He said the word hesitantly. "For a minute, you didn't feel like…" He decided not to finish the thought. He didn't want to concern her. Not until he understood what was going on with the girl.

"What, Sebastian? Feel like what?"

"Nothing." He sat up, felt inside his pocket and found the locket still there. He pulled it out and stared at the scrolling A on the front. Round and gold and a bit dinged-up. The only thing special about it was its sentimentality. Sebastian opened it, sought the pictures Alice kept close to her heart.

Sebastian stared at the open locket exposed in his palm. Stared at the miniature tracking device expertly placed within.

Shit.

He dropped the locket on the bedside table.

Shit. Shit. Shit.

That was how Davies and his men had found Sebastian and Kyra in the park. Were they tracking them even now? Tracking them all the way to the carnival? Could Jon Davies and his group of soldiers find a portal to lead the way?

Sebastian lifted his table lamp and slammed it down on the locket with a mighty force, smashing the tracker to bits. He looked up at Chelsea's stunned face. "You said Kyra was outside?" He stood and walked right past Chelsea, out the door of his trailer into the night beyond.

Kyra leaned against the wall of the trailer, watching the lights of the carnival. She looked cozy wrapped in her sweater, hands cocooned within the sleeves. At the same time, she looked heartbreakingly distant, lost in thought.

"So, you found your way back to the carnival," he said, hopeful of what this meant for her memory.

Kyra jumped at the sound of his voice, then turned to face him, her face bright with surprise. "You had me worried."

"No worries. See? I'm fine." Sebastian spread his hands to the side to emphasize how fine he was. And he was fine. Never felt better.

Kyra bit her lip and nodded.

Sebastian took a step closer. Familiar with her many faces, he could tell something bothered her. He wanted to know what gnawed at her now. "Your mom's here?"

"Apparently my dad told her where to find me." She chewed on her lower lip before continuing. "You wouldn't know anything about that, would you?" Sebastian shrugged, but said nothing. Kyra rolled her head. "This whole thing with Marcus has her agitated. She says it's time. Time for me to make a decision. Do you remember anything about that?" Kyra gnawed on her fingernails.

Sebastian's brow tightened, weighed down, narrowing his sight. "You don't?"

"Not really. Vaguely. I remember very little."

"But you remembered the carnival. You got us back here safely." He glanced around, feeling a fog of confusion. He noticed Chelsea walking away from the trailer, a bit of huff to her step.

Knew there was something about her, something he should be following up on, but he was with Kyra now.

"I didn't remember the carnival," Kyra said. "I was running after my mom. She had you, and I didn't want to lose either one of you. Next thing I knew, we were falling through another one of those things you took me through earlier. A portal, you called it. We ended up here. My mom was not happy, but some old guy—I think his name was Zeke?—he said the carnival brought us here because this was where we were supposed to be." Kyra looked after Chelsea and pointed. "That blonde girl showed us to your place and we got you situated." Kyra moved in closer, so close their noses were mere inches apart. "She has a thing for you."

"I wouldn't go that far," Sebastian said and tilted his head, exploring the side of Kyra, memorizing her. "And your dragon? You have water and fire. What will you do?"

Kyra inched closer still. He could feel her breath on his skin. "That's the thing. I can't feel my dragon. I don't know if I can do anything."

Sebastian felt the tension yank up his spine like a coaster car making the ride's first climb. "Are you still cold?"

Kyra nodded and pulled her long sweater closed tight around her.

He shook his head. "That doesn't make sense. I saw Kalrapura. We saw Kalrapura. Didn't you feel the blast of her return?"

Kyra shrugged. "I admit I felt something. But to be honest, all I've been able to think about since the day you showed up at my door is you."

Sebastian turned away. "None of this makes any sense. I cut you to draw Kalrapura back to you."

Kyra tugged at his arm, pulled him back. "How was that supposed to work, exactly?"

He raked his hand through his hair. Dammit. Why hadn't it worked? What had he done wrong? He looked up and met her gaze. "The blood, of course. It's your blood she should be drawn to first. Above all others."

Kyra bit her lip and nodded.

"Yeah, I. Just don't—" He stammered, then remembered. "The tooth pendant. Are you still wearing it? Maybe it's working to suppress her, somehow?"

"What tooth pendant?"

"The one Marcus gave you. You used to wear it before…" Sebastian hesitated.

"Before I lost my memory?" Kyra finished.

He nodded, one quick tilt of the head.

"I haven't seen anything like what you speak of."

Sebastian's brow furrowed and he rubbed at his forehead with his thumb and forefingers. He'd thought it all out so carefully. Where was Kalrapura?

Kyra placed her hand along his cheek and looked deep into his eyes. Her touch was one of warmth and sincerity. "It's alright. We'll figure this thing out together. I have faith in you. In us."

Sebastian cracked half a smile. He wanted to really smile, but in the last hour things had gone from bad to oh-crap. Now he had some serious Mara hunters on his ass, and for the first time he realized something. "I need my dad."

"What?" Kyra startled.

Sebastian had surprised even himself. "I need to better understand myself if I'm going to protect us from this new threat in our lives. In order to do that, I'll need my dad."

"Ah, okay." Kyra wrapped her arms around him. Sebastian straightened and gazed into her eyes. "I thought," she paused and sighed, "or hoped, you didn't want anything to do with him?"

"I don't, but I'm gonna have to look past that for now."

"You're doing that for us?"

Sebastian bowed his head slightly.

"I don't know how things were between us before I lost my memory, but I know how I want them to be now." Kyra's fingers brushed along the edge of his lips.

"How is that?" Sebastian's hand skimmed along the curve of her neck, slipping up along her jawline, the delicate edge of her ear.

No further words were spoken. Words were unnecessary to express their feelings regarding each other. Their bodies melded into one, her light enveloping his darkness. His night complementing her day. He was cold where she was warmth. They were yin and yang, opposites fitting together in perfect concord and tranquility.

Her dragon raced through him, burned him, and he knew they would solve the puzzle. Kalrapura was there. He could sense her, feel her. Together they would bring her to the surface.

Their kiss was all he had hoped for in a true first kiss, and what he never dreamed they would have. Every part of him—his body, his soul—longed for her. His limbs burned for her. The fire shot through his system like a hellhound on a vengeance mission. He wanted to scream. He only kissed her harder, deeper.

He never knew desire could hurt this way. It prickled across his back and spine, pushing out, wanting more. More Kyra. More everything. He was consumed by her, burned for her.

"Sebastian!"

He heard the scream. Once. Then again. He opened his eyes.

Kyra was on top of him. He was laid out on the ground. His hands were scorched and flames burned from his fingertips. She beat him with a rag. Massive wings, riddled with holes, wrapped out around him.

"She's in you. The dragon is inside you!" Kyra yelled, and continued to beat at the fire.

No. Sebastian stared up at the night. Somehow, somewhere, something had gone terribly wrong. Could he fix the mistake? Or would he forever be a Reaper and a Mara—and a Dragon?

The End

BEFORE YOU GO...

Dear Reader,

I hope you enjoyed *Plight of the Dragon*. Thank you so much for coming along on Kyra and Sebastian's adventure. I had a blast writing their story! I did it for them and for you—the reader. Will there be more to their story? Hard to say. You tell me how badly you want to read what's next in their whirlwind of a supernatural-carnie love story. It just might inspire what comes next. It's the readers and reviewers who make up the foundation of our author world, and we love you madly for all you do! That being said, I have to ask a favor of you, if you don't mind. I'd like to invite you to post a review of the book on Amazon or Goodreads. Not only do I love receiving feedback, but reviews also help other readers find what they are looking for.

Thanks! Until next time, keep the magic real.

Debra Kristi

. . . .

For updates about new releases, as well as exclusive promotions and giveaways, sign up for Debra Kristi's Insider's Club mailing list here:

http://eepurl.com/T3tNv

I'D LOVE TO CONNECT! FIND ME HERE:

Debra Kristi's Immortal Warriors: my private Facebook fan group. Come join us there. This is where the good stuff happens. Discussion on books, on life, and exclusive giveaways and promotions just for Debra Kristi Immortal Warrior fans: **https://www.facebook.com/groups/1641310842822994/**

Discover more about me and my books on my website: **http://www.debrakristi.com/**

Debra Kristi's Facebook author page: updates, news, discussions, and more: **https://www.facebook.com/DebraKristi.writer/**

Pinterest: boards and pictures about everything from storyboards to fantasy worlds to people and places I love. Come join in the pinning fun: **https://www.pinterest.com/debrakristi/**

Join the YA Book Love & Discuss Pinterest Board and talk books: **https://www.pinterest.com/debrakristi/ya-book-love-discuss/**

Instagram: pictures of books and cats. Two things I can't get enough of. Stop by: **https://instagram.com/debrakristi/**

Twitter: @debrakristi **https://twitter.com/DebraKristi**

Tumblr: My geek side, books, and more: **http://debrakristi.tumblr.com/**

Email me directly at **debra@debrakristi.com**

The *Age of the Hybrid* Series is a story within the Mystic's Carnival Collective (MCC)—a collection of stories sharing a common world written by various authors. If this is your first visit to the collective and you would like to explore more, please visit mysticscarnival.com. Like a real carnival, there are many tents to explore and worlds to discover, just inside the gates. All you have to do is step through.

ACKNOWLEDGMENTS

Most importantly, I need to thank you—the reader! You are awesome and my stories would be lonely without you. You are everything.

I wouldn't have made it this far without the amazing team that helped sharpen and shine this fantastical story. You guys rock! Thanks to my tireless editors: Tiffany Turpin Johnson of TJ Writeography, and Shelly Tegen and Holly Kammier of Acorn Editing. Love you guys! Faith Williams of the Atwater Group, hugs! I need you in my corner. And for piecing it all together and making it pop, thank you a thousand times over, Adara Rosalie and Melinda VanLone!

Betas!! You guys are the best! Love you to pieces: Kristy K. James, Lynne Freeman, and Diana Beebe. To my family—I couldn't be more blessed. I am forever indebted to you. Love you all so much.

GLOSSARY OF TERMS

Essence of Anodynse – The incense extracted from the spinal fluid of dragons.

Balidhug – The name by which Marcus is referred to by those not in his circle.

Behemoth – Supernatural beasts, chaos monsters the size of rhinoceros.

Bolsvck – The rightful Fire Dragon King who refused to rule—Kyra's father.

Chaos Demon – Destructive Demons born from the earth and out of chaos.

Convergence – Merging and resurfacing of lost species with one vessel.

Dragonet – The equivalent of a teen dragon.

Dragonling – A baby dragon.

Gatekeeper – A race of men and women responsible for determining location, creation, and maintaining the portals between worlds.

Grim Reaper – A member of the Reaper class who has ascended to the top rank.

Hellhound – A supernatural dog with black spiked fur, yellow eyes, tremendous speed and strength, thought to guard a rare, supernatural treasure.

Infraction 183 – Failure to comply with a superior Grim Reaper.

Kalrapura – The name of Kyra's dragon.

Mara Web – A web used to trap and confine a Mara. Turns the Mara's powers in upon her or himself.

Minor Reaper – A member of the Reaper class who is undergoing the learning process, working beneath a Grim Reaper's supervision.

Mobürn – Home land of the Fire Dragons.

Moorigad – The blending of two dragon species. The traits of both parents clashed within the host fighting for control.

Purgatory – The limbo state between Heaven and Hell.

Rajūn – the first dragon and great water deity.

Spiritual Peace – A witch's brew allowing a Reaper to escape his or her mental and memory gathering gift.

Zilant – A winged, snake-like creature. Cousin to the dragon.

If you enjoyed following Kyra and Sebastian's story through books one and two of the Age of the Hybrid, read the epic conclusion in:

Book 3 in the Age of the Hybrid Series
A Mystic's Carnival Story

PLIGHT OF THE DRAGON

DEBRA KRISTI

PLIGHT OF THE DRAGON

GLIMPSE

Sebastian flailed on the damp ground, thrashing his arms into the mud, the flames licking at his skin. Excruciating, his mind screamed. In reality, it merely tickled, but his brain could not comprehend the meaning—not yet, anyway.

The luminescence and sparkle provided by the trailers, signs, and wizardry wonders found in Mystic's Magical Market, his little home and pocket of fortunetellers and wannabes within the supernatural destination known as Mystic's Carnival, was lost to him now. There was only the chaos, and fire.

Kyra batted and slapped and hit him with her hands. It didn't hurt. Her touch comforted, reassured Sebastian he still mattered in her world. The image of her danced before him like a moth losing survival's fight to the fire: exquisite flickers of orange and red, death courting life's essence. His vision impaired, bleaching a rainbow of colors from his sight, he stared through a filter of senseless heat and anger. And everything around him, absolutely everything, smelled of burning and ash.

The word dragon slithered around the bends and folds of his grey matter. In the earlier struggle, he and Kyra had retrieved Kyra's dragon half, Kalrapura. They'd saved her from Marcus. From being devoured or absorbed for his malicious scheme. But in returning her to Kyra, they had failed. How in Hell's Gates had the dragon ended up inside Sebastian?

Kyra's words crashed back into his thoughts. She's in you. The dragon is inside you!

His skin charred from his fingertips toward the bend of his elbow. His back shook with spasms, then exploded in torment, slicing from his shoulders down the sides of his spine, ripping the fabric of his shirt. Massive wings, salmon-colored and torn, swung from behind him and around Kyra. They curled up then flapped out of sight, before reappearing at her side again. Sebastian tried to focus, not on the wings, but on Kyra. It was difficult. His mind swirled with emotion, and she remained unclear, washed in tones of crimson quivering with gold. What if scales started to replace his skin? Or the man he was ceased to be?

"Calm yourself." Her steady gaze eased his physical madness, and her voice swam through his head straight to his heart, releasing the iron lock around his internal peace. She was the medicine he needed, and he would let her guide him. He knew nothing about the condition he now faced.

Pushing his arms to the side and abandoning the burn of his hands, Kyra straddled him and lowered her face close to his own. The distance between them was mere inches, and even after all they had been through, the scent of sunflowers still lingered on her skin. He remembered the sunflowers in Marcus's apartment, the smell wafting around her at the coffee shop. She'd said she was cold, that the flowers gave her the illusion of warmth. Her physiology was probably built to balance the strength and heat a dragon radiated. Without the dragon's fire, she was chilled. He, on the other hand, not meant to harbor such a beast, was burning to cinders.

Her palms cupped his cheeks, and they exchanged endless dialogue through their gaze, no word spoken aloud. Kyra's stare bore straight to Sebastian's soul. His breath froze, and his heart skittered…and he felt the dragon coil.

"Control can only be found in the calm of one's own mind." She touched her forehead to his. "Search and find yours."

Her words washed over him like the healing waters of serenity. The warmth of her skin, the gentle caress of her hands along the curve of his jawline—instant tranquility.

The wild flapping of wings subsided. The throbbing in his back dulled. And the flickering heat of fire burning inside him abated. Sebastian was almost himself again…or at least looked the part. He no longer displayed any uniquely dragon features. He took a deep breath. So deep it reached into his gut, tried to claw at the core of his being. He wished he could will the dragon back to her. Will it through their touch. But nothing was ever that simple.

In the span of a few days, his life had been shredded and taped back together in a special kind of horror.

They might have saved Kyra's dragon, but they hadn't stopped the ceremony. Marcus now had the strength and power of multiple dragons running through his veins, had a small army at his beck and call, and wanted Sebastian dead. On top of that, some kind of rebel military force had targeted Sebastian as enemy number one for the deaths of two fallen comrades, two deaths Sebastian had not caused. He had his father Mortifier to thank for that one. Then there was an insane Mara after him for her personal breeding stock. If that weren't just ghastly gross. Not gonna happen.

But now…now he had a dragon trapped inside of him. An all-powerful, beastly, hybrid dragon, inside of him, a Reaper! What did that make him? A reaping dragon?

Sebastian sighed and closed his eyes. At least Kyra had returned to him.

He opened his eyes and gazed up at her. He could see forever and back. She was his now, his tomorrow, his for all days until the end. The end of time, or the end of him. Kyra was, and would always be, his everything.

Two arms hooked under Kyra's armpits, lifted her up and away. And just like that, she was gone.

to be continued...

ABOUT THE AUTHOR

 Debra Kristi was born and raised a Southern California girl. She still resides in the sunny state with her husband, two kids, and four schizophrenic cats. Her love for the fantastical began at a very young age, when her imagination magically transformed the backyard swing set into the U.S.S. Enterprise. Since then she's had a lifelong love of science fiction, fantasy, and creative storytelling. Unlike the characters she often writes, Debra is not immortal and her only superpower is letting the dishes and laundry pile up.

When not writing or chatting it up on social media, Debra is hanging out creating priceless memories with her family, geeking out to science fiction and fantasy television, and tossing around movie quotes.

www.ingramcontent.com/pod-product-compliance
Lightning Source LLC
Chambersburg PA
CBHW051845170626
46807CB00003B/1364